The truth is rarely pure and never simple. Modern life would be very tedious if it were either, and modern literature a complete impossibility.

1 3 5 7 9 10 8 6 4 2

Vintage
20 Vauxhall Bridge Road,
London SW1V 2SA

Vintage Classics is part of the Penguin Random House
group of companies whose addresses can be found at
global.penguinrandomhouse.com

Penguin
Random House
UK

This edition published by Vintage in 2020

penguin.co.uk/vintage

A CIP catalogue record for this book is available from the British Library

ISBN 9781784876074

Typeset in 10.5/14.5 pt FreightText Pro
by Jouve (UK), Milton Keynes
Printed and bound in Great Britain by Clays Ltd, Elcograf S.p.A.

Penguin Random House is committed to a sustainable future for our
business, our readers and our planet. This book is made from Forest
Stewardship Council® certified paper.

MIX
Paper from
responsible sources
FSC® C018179
www.fsc.org

Lies

OSCAR WILDE

VINTAGE MINIS

Contents

1

The Importance of Being Earnest

ACT ONE

Morning-room in ALGERNON's *flat in Half-Moon Street. The room is luxuriously and artistically furnished. The sound of a piano is heard in the adjoining room.* LANE *is arranging afternoon tea on the table; after the music has ceased,* ALGERNON *enters.*

Enter LANE.

LANE: Mr Ernest Worthing.

Enter JACK. LANE *goes out.*

ALGERNON: How are you, my dear Ernest? What brings you up to town?

JACK: Oh, pleasure, pleasure! What else should bring one anywhere? Eating as usual, I see, Algy!

ALGERNON (*stiffly*): I believe it is customary in good society to take some slight refreshment at five o'clock. Where have you been since last Thursday?

JACK (*smiling and sitting down on the sofa*): In the country.

ALGERNON: What on earth do you do there?

JACK (*pulling off his gloves*): When one is in town one amuses oneself. When one is in the country one amuses other people. It is excessively boring.

ALGERNON: And who are the people you amuse?

JACK (*airily*): Oh, neighbours, neighbours.

ALGERNON: Got nice neighbours in your part of Shropshire?

JACK: Perfectly horrid! Never speak to one of them.

ALGERNON: How immensely you must amuse them! (*goes over and takes sandwich*) By the way, Shropshire is your county, is it not?

JACK: Eh? Shropshire? Yes, of course. Hallo! Why all these cups? Why cucumber sandwiches? Why such reckless extravagance in one so young? Who is coming to tea?

ALGERNON: Oh! merely Aunt Augusta and Gwendolen.

JACK: How perfectly delightful!

ALGERNON: Yes, that is all very well; but I am afraid Aunt Augusta won't quite approve of your being here.

JACK: May I ask why?

ALGERNON: My dear fellow, the way you flirt with Gwendolen is perfectly disgraceful. It is almost as bad as the way Gwendolen flirts with you.

JACK: I am in love with Gwendolen. I have come up to town expressly to propose to her.

ALGERNON: I thought you had come up for pleasure? . . . I call that business.

JACK: How utterly unromantic you are!

ALGERNON: I really don't see anything romantic in proposing. It is very romantic to be in love. But there is nothing romantic about a definite proposal. Why, one may be accepted. One usually is, I believe. Then the excitement is all over. The very essence of romance is uncertainty. If ever I get married, I'll certainly try to forget the fact.

JACK: I have no doubt about that, dear Algy. The divorce court was specially invented for people whose memories are so curiously constituted.

ALGERNON: Oh! there is no use speculating on that subject. Divorces are made in heaven – (JACK *puts out his hand to take a sandwich.* ALGERNON *at once interferes*) Please don't touch the cucumber sandwiches. They are ordered specially for Aunt Augusta. (*takes one and eats it*)

JACK: Well, you have been eating them all the time.

ALGERNON: That is quite a different matter. She is my aunt. (*takes plate from below*) Have some bread and butter. The bread and butter is for Gwendo-len. Gwendolen is devoted to bread and butter.

JACK (*advancing to table and helping himself*): And very good bread and butter it is too.

ALGERNON: Well, my dear fellow, you need not eat as if you were going to eat it all. You behave as if you were married to her already. You are not married to her already, and I don't think you ever will be.

JACK: Why on earth do you say that?

ALGERNON: Well, in the first place girls never marry the men they flirt with. Girls don't think it right.

JACK: Oh, that is nonsense!

ALGERNON: It isn't. It is a great truth. It accounts for the extraordinary number of bachelors that one sees all over the place. In the second place, I don't give my consent.

JACK: Your consent!

ALGERNON: My dear fellow, Gwendolen is my first cousin. And before I allow you to marry her, you will have to clear up the whole question of Cecily. (*rings bell*)

JACK: Cecily! What on earth do you mean? What do you mean, Algy, by Cecily! I don't know anyone of the name of Cecily.

Enter LANE.

ALGERNON: Bring me that cigarette case Mr Worthing left in the smoking-room the last time he dined here.

LANE: Yes, sir.

LANE goes out.

JACK: Do you mean to say you have had my cigarette case all this time? I wish to goodness you had let me know. I have been writing frantic letters to Scotland Yard about it. I was very nearly offering a large reward.

ALGERNON: Well, I wish you would offer one. I happen to be more than usually hard up.

JACK: There is no good offering a large reward now that the thing is found.

Enter LANE with the cigarette case on a salver.
ALGERNON takes it at once. LANE goes out.

ALGERNON: I think that is rather mean of you, Ernest, I must say. (*opens case and examines it*) However, it makes no matter, for, now that I look at the inscription inside, I find that the thing isn't yours after all.

JACK: Of course it's mine. (*moving to him*) You have seen me with it a hundred times, and you have no right whatsoever to read what is written inside. It is a very ungentlemanly thing to read a private cigarette case.

ALGERNON: Oh! it is absurd to have a hard and fast rule about what one should read and what one shouldn't. More than half of modern culture depends on what one shouldn't read.

JACK: I am quite aware of the fact, and I don't propose to discuss modern culture. It isn't the sort of thing one should talk of in private. I simply want my cigarette case back.

ALGERNON: Yes; but this isn't your cigarette case. This cigarette case is a present from someone of the name of Cecily, and you said you didn't know anyone of that name.

JACK: Well, if you want to know, Cecily happens to be my aunt.

ALGERNON: Your aunt!

JACK: Yes. Charming old lady she is, too. Lives at Tunbridge Wells. Just give it back to me, Algy.

ALGERNON (*retreating to back of sofa*): But why does she call herself little Cecily if she is your aunt and lives at Tunbridge Wells? (*reading*) 'From little Cecily, with her fondest love.'

JACK (*moving to sofa and kneeling upon it*): My dear fellow what on earth is there in that? Some aunts are tall, some aunts are not tall. That is a matter that surely an aunt may be allowed to decide for herself. You seem to think that every aunt should be exactly like your aunt! That is absurd! For heaven's sake give me back my cigarette case. (*follows* ALGERNON *round the room*)

ALGERNON: Yes. But why does your aunt call you her uncle? 'From little Cecily, with her fondest love to her dear Uncle Jack.' There is no objection, I admit, to an aunt being a small aunt, but why an aunt, no matter what her size may be, should call her own nephew her uncle, I can't quite make out. Besides, your name isn't Jack at all; it is Ernest.

JACK: It isn't Ernest; it's Jack.

ALGERNON: You have always told me it was Ernest. I have introduced you to everyone as Ernest. You answer to the name of Ernest. You look as if your name was Ernest. You are the most earnest-looking person I ever saw in my life. It is perfectly absurd your saying that your name isn't Ernest. It's on your cards. Here is one of them. (*taking it from case*) 'Mr Ernest Worthing, B4, Albany'. I'll keep this as a proof that your name is Ernest if ever you attempt to deny it to me, or to Gwendolen, or to anyone else. (*puts the card in his pocket*)

JACK: Well, my name is Ernest in town and Jack in the country, and the cigarette case was given to me in the country.

ALGERNON: Yes, but that does not account for the fact that your small Aunt Cecily, who lives at Tunbridge Wells, calls you her dear uncle. Come, old boy, you had much better have the thing out at once.

JACK: My dear Algy, you talk exactly as if you were a dentist. It is very vulgar to talk like a dentist when one isn't a dentist. It produces a false impression.

ALGERNON: Well, that is exactly what dentists always do. Now, go on! Tell me the whole thing. I may mention that I have always suspected you of being a confirmed and secret Bunburyist; and I am quite sure of it now.

JACK: Bunburyist? What on earth do you mean by a Bunburyist?

ALGERNON: I'll reveal to you the meaning of that incomparable expression as soon as you are kind enough to inform me why you are Ernest in town and Jack in the country.

JACK: Well, produce my cigarette case first.

ALGERNON: Here it is. (*hands cigarette case*) Now produce your explanation, and pray make it improbable. (*sits on sofa*)

JACK: My dear fellow, there is nothing improbable about my explanation at all. In fact, it's perfectly ordinary. Old Mr Thomas Cardew, who adopted me when I was a little boy, made me in his will guardian to his granddaughter, Miss Cecily Cardew. Cecily, who addresses me as her uncle from motives of respect that you could not possibly appreciate, lives at my place in the country under the charge of her admirable governess, Miss Prism.

ALGERNON: Where is that place in the country, by the way?

JACK: That is nothing to you, dear boy. You are not going to be invited . . . I may tell you candidly that the place is not in Shropshire.

ALGERNON: I suspected that, my dear fellow! I have Bunburyed all over Shropshire on two separate occasions. Now, go on. Why are you Ernest in town and Jack in the country?

JACK: My dear Algy, I don't know whether you will be able to understand my real motives. You are hardly serious enough. When one is placed in the position of guardian, one has to adopt a very high moral tone on all subjects. It's one's duty to do so. And as a high moral tone can hardly be said to conduce very much to either one's health or one's happiness, in order to get up to town I have always pretended to have a younger brother of the name of Ernest, who lives in the Albany, and gets into the most dreadful scrapes. That, my dear Algy, is the whole truth pure and simple.

ALGERNON: The truth is rarely pure and never simple. Modern life would be very tedious if it were either, and modern literature a complete impossibility!

JACK: That wouldn't be at all a bad thing.

ALGERNON: Literary criticism is not your forte, my dear fellow. Don't try it. You should leave that to people who haven't been at a university. They do it so well in the daily papers. What you really are is a Bunburyist. I was quite right in saying you were a Bunburyist. You are one of the most advanced Bunburyists I know.

JACK: What an earth do you mean?

ALGERNON: You have invented a very useful younger brother called Ernest, in order that you may be able to come up to town as often as you like. I have invented an invaluable permanent invalid called Bunbury, in order that I may be able to go down into the country whenever I choose. Bunbury is perfectly invaluable. If it wasn't for Bunbury's extraordinary bad health, for instance, I wouldn't be able to dine with you at Willis's tonight, for I have been really engaged to Aunt Augusta for more than a week.

JACK: I haven't asked you to dine with me anywhere tonight.

ALGERNON: I know. You are absurdly careless about sending out invitations. It is very foolish of you. Nothing annoys people so much as not receiving invitations.

JACK: You had much better dine with your Aunt Augusta.

ALGERNON: I haven't the smallest intention of doing anything of the kind. To begin with, I dined there on Monday, and once a week is quite enough to dine with one's own relations. In the second place, whenever I do dine there I am always treated as a member of the family, and sent down with either no woman at all, or two. In the third place, I know perfectly well whom she will place me next to, tonight. She will place me next to Mary Farquhar, who always flirts with her own husband across the dinner-table. That is not very pleasant. Indeed, it is not even decent . . . and that sort of thing is enormously on the increase. The amount of women in London who flirt with their own husbands is perfectly scandalous. It looks so bad. It is simply washing one's clean linen in public. Besides, now that I know you to be a confirmed Bunburyist I naturally want to talk to you about Bunburying. I want to tell you the rules.

JACK: I'm not a Bunburyist at all. If Gwendolen accepts me, I am going to kill my brother, indeed I think I'll kill him in any case. Cecily is a little too much interested in him. It is rather a bore. So I am going to get rid of Ernest. And I strongly advise you to do the same with Mr . . . with your invalid friend who has the absurd name.

ALGERNON: Nothing will induce me to part with Bunbury, and if you ever get married, which seems to me extremely problematic, you will be very glad to know Bunbury. A man who marries without knowing Bunbury has a very tedious time of it.

JACK: That is nonsense. If I marry a charming girl like Gwendolen, and she is the only girl I ever saw in my life that I would marry, I certainly won't want to know Bunbury.

ALGERNON: Then your wife will. You don't seem to realise, that in married life three is company and two is none.

JACK (*sententiously*): That, my dear young friend, is the theory that the corrupt French drama has been propounding for the last fifty years.

ALGERNON: Yes; and that the happy English home has proved in half the time.

JACK: For heaven's sake, don't try to be cynical. It's perfectly easy to be cynical.

ALGERNON: My dear fellow, it isn't easy to be anything nowadays. There's such a lot of beastly competition about. (*the sound of an electric bell is heard*) Ah! that must be Aunt Augusta. Only relatives, or creditors, ever ring in that Wagnerian manner. Now, if I get her out of the way for ten minutes, so that you can have an opportunity for proposing to Gwendolen, may I dine with you tonight at Willis's?

JACK: I suppose so, if you want to.

ALGERNON: Yes, but you must be serious about it. I hate people who are not serious about meals. It is so shallow of them.

Enter LANE.

LANE: Lady Bracknell and Miss Fairfax.

ALGERNON *goes forward to meet them. Enter* LADY
BRACKNELL *and* GWENDOLEN.

LADY BRACKNELL: Good afternoon, dear Algernon,
I hope you are behaving very well.

ALGERNON: I'm feeling very well, Aunt Augusta.

LADY BRACKNELL: That's not quite the same thing.
In fact the two things rarely go together. (*sees*
JACK *and bows to him with icy coldness*)

ALGERNON (*to* GWENDOLEN): Dear me, you are smart!

GWENDOLEN: I am always smart! Am I not, Mr
Worthing?

JACK: You're quite perfect, Miss Fairfax.

GWENDOLEN: Oh! I hope I am not that. It would
leave no room for developments, and I intend to
develop in many directions. (GWENDOLEN *and*
JACK *sit down together in the corner*)

LADY BRACKNELL: I'm sorry if we are a little late,
Algernon, but I was obliged to call on dear Lady
Harbury. I hadn't been there since her poor husband's death. I never saw a woman so altered; she
looks quite twenty years younger. And now I'll
have a cup of tea, and one of those nice cucumber
sandwiches you promised me.

ALGERNON: Certainly, Aunt Augusta. (*goes over to tea-table*)

LADY BRACKNELL: Won't you come and sit here, Gwendolen?

GWENDOLEN: Thanks, mamma, I'm quite comfortable where I am.

ALGERNON (*picking up empty plate in horror*): Good heavens! Lane! Why are there no cucumber sandwiches? I ordered them specially.

LANE (*gravely*): There were no cucumbers in the market this morning, sir. I went down twice.

ALGERNON: No cucumbers!

LANE: No, sir. Not even for ready money.

ALGERNON: That will do, Lane, thank you.

LANE: Thank you, sir. (*goes out*)

ALGERNON: I am greatly distressed, Aunt Augusta, about there being no cucumbers, not even for ready money.

LADY BRACKNELL: It really makes no matter, Algernon. I had some crumpets with Lady Harbury, who seems to me to be living entirely for pleasure now.

ALGERNON: I hear her hair has turned quite gold from grief.

LADY BRACKNELL: It certainly has changed its colour. From what cause I, of course, cannot say. (ALGERNON *crosses and hands tea*) Thank you. I've quite a treat for you tonight, Algernon. I am going to send you down with Mary Farquhar. She is such a nice woman and so attentive to her husband. It's delightful to watch them.

ALGERNON: I am afraid, Aunt Augusta, I shall have to give up the pleasure of dining with you tonight after all.

LADY BRACKNELL (*frowning*): I hope not, Algernon. It would put my table completely out. Your uncle would have to dine upstairs. Fortunately he is accustomed to that.

ALGERNON: It is a great bore, and, I need hardly say, a terrible disappointment to me, but the fact is I have just had a telegram to say that my poor friend Bunbury is very ill again. (*exchanges glances with* JACK) They seem to think I should be with him.

LADY BRACKNELL: It is very strange. This Mr Bunbury seems to suffer from curiously bad health.

ALGERNON: Yes; poor Bunbury is a dreadful invalid.

LADY BRACKNELL: Well, I must say, Algernon, that I think it is high time that Mr Bunbury made up his mind whether he was going to live or to die. This shilly-shallying with the question is absurd. Nor do I in any way approve of the modern sympathy with invalids. I consider it morbid. Illness of any kind is hardly a thing to be encouraged in others. Health is the primary duty of life. I am always telling that to your poor uncle, but he never seems to take much notice ... as far as any improvement in his ailment goes. I should be much obliged if you would ask Mr Bunbury, from me, to be kind enough not to have a relapse on Saturday, for I rely on you to arrange my music for me. It is my last reception, and one wants something that will encourage conversation, particularly at the end of the season when everyone has practically said whatever they had to say, which, in most cases, was probably not much.

ALGERNON: I'll speak to Bunbury, Aunt Augusta, if he is still conscious, and I think I can promise you he'll be all right by Saturday. Of course the music is a great difficulty. You see, if one plays good music, people don't listen, and if one plays bad music people don't talk. But I'll run over the programme I've drawn out, if you will kindly come into the next room for a moment.

LADY BRACKNELL: Thank you, Algernon. It is very thoughtful of you. (*rising, and following* ALGERNON) I'm sure the programme will be delightful, after a few expurgations. French songs I cannot possibly allow. People always seem to think that they are improper, and either look shocked, which is vulgar, or laugh, which is worse. But German sounds a thoroughly respectable language, and indeed, I believe is so. Gwendolen, you will accompany me.

GWENDOLEN: Certainly, mamma.

LADY BRACKNELL *and* ALGERNON *go into the music-room,* GWENDOLEN *remains behind.*

JACK: Charming day it has been, Miss Fairfax.

GWENDOLEN: Pray don't talk to me about the weather, Mr Worthing. Whenever people talk to me about the weather, I always feel quite certain that they mean something else. And that makes me so nervous.

JACK: I do mean something else.

GWENDOLEN: I thought so. In fact, I am never wrong.

JACK: And I would like to be allowed to take advantage of Lady Bracknell's temporary absence . . .

GWENDOLEN: I would certainly advise you to do so. Mamma has a way of coming back suddenly into a room that I have often had to speak to her about.

JACK (*nervously*): Miss Fairfax, ever since I met you I have admired you more than any girl I have ever met since . . . I met you.

GWENDOLEN: Yes, I am quite well aware of the fact. And I often wish that in public, at any rate, you had been more demonstrative. For me you have always had an irresistible fascination. Even before I met you I was far from indifferent to you. (JACK *looks at her in amazement*) We live, as I hope you know, Mr Worthing, in an age of ideals. The fact is constantly mentioned in the more expensive monthly magazines, and has reached the provincial pulpits, I am told; and my ideal has always been to love someone of the name of Ernest. There is something in that name that inspires absolute

confidence. The moment Algernon first mentioned to me that he had a friend called Ernest, I
knew I was destined to love you.

JACK: You really love me, Gwendolen?

GWENDOLEN: Passionately!

JACK: Darling! You don't know how happy you've
made me.

GWENDOLEN: My own Ernest!

JACK: But you don't really mean to say that you
couldn't love me if my name wasn't Ernest?

GWENDOLEN: But your name is Ernest.

JACK: Yes, I know it is. But supposing it was something else? Do you mean to say you couldn't love
me then?

GWENDOLEN (*glibly*): Ah! that is clearly a metaphysical speculation, and like most metaphysical specu-
lations has very little reference at all to the actual
facts of real life, as we know them.

JACK: Personally, darling, to speak quite candidly, I
don't much care about the name of Ernest . . .
I don't think the name suits me at all.

GWENDOLEN: It suits you perfectly. It is a divine name.
It has a music of its own. It produces vibrations.

JACK: Well, really, Gwendolen, I must say that I think
there are lots of other much nicer names. I think
Jack, for instance, a charming name.

GWENDOLEN: Jack? . . . No, there is very little music
in the name Jack, if any at all, indeed. It does not

thrill. It produces absolutely no vibrations . . . I have known several Jacks, and they all, without exception, were more than usually plain. Besides, Jack is a notorious domesticity for John! And I pity any woman who is married to a man called John. She would probably never be allowed to know the entrancing pleasure of a single moment's solitude. The only really safe name is Ernest.

JACK: Gwendolen, I must get christened at once – I mean we must get married at once. There is no time to be lost.

GWENDOLEN: Married, Mr Worthing?

JACK (*astounded*): Well . . . surely. You know that I love you, and you led me to believe, Miss Fairfax, that you were not absolutely indifferent to me.

GWENDOLEN: I adore you. But you haven't proposed to me yet. Nothing has been said at all about marriage. The subject has not even been touched on.

JACK: Well . . . may I propose to you now?

GWENDOLEN: I think it would be an admirable opportunity. And to spare you any possible disappointment, Mr Worthing, I think it only fair to tell you quite frankly beforehand that I am fully determined to accept you.

JACK: Gwendolen!

GWENDOLEN: Yes, Mr Worthing, what have you got to say to me?

JACK: You know what I have got to say to you.

GWENDOLEN: Yes, but you don't say it.

JACK: Gwendolen, will you marry me? (*goes on his knees*)

GWENDOLEN: Of course I will, darling. How long you have been about it! I am afraid you have had very little experience in how to propose.

JACK: My own one, I have never loved anyone in the world but you.

GWENDOLEN: Yes, but men often propose for practice. I know my brother Gerald does. All my girlfriends tell me so. What wonderfully blue eyes you have, Ernest! They are quite, quite, blue. I hope you will always look at me just like that, especially when there are other people present.

Enter LADY BRACKNELL.

LADY BRACKNELL: Mr Worthing! Rise, sir, from this semi-recumbent posture. It is most indecorous.

GWENDOLEN: Mamma! (*he tries to rise; she restrains him*) I must beg you to retire. This is no place for you. Besides Mr Worthing has not quite finished yet.

LADY BRACKNELL: Finished what, may I ask?

GWENDOLEN: I am engaged to Mr Worthing, mamma. (*they rise together*)

LADY BRACKNELL: Pardon me, you are not engaged to anyone. When you do become engaged to someone, I, or your father, should his health permit him, will inform you of the fact. An engagement should come on a young girl as a surprise, pleasant or unpleasant, as the case may be. It is hardly a matter that she could be allowed to arrange for herself . . . And now, I have a few questions to put to you, Mr Worthing. While I am making these enquiries, you, Gwendolen, will wait for me below in the carriage.

GWENDOLEN (*reproachfully*): Mamma!

LADY BRACKNELL: In the carriage, Gwendolen!

GWENDOLEN *goes to the door. She and* JACK *blow kisses to each other behind* LADY BRACKNELL'*s back.* LADY BRACKNELL *looks vaguely about as if she could not understand what the noise was. Finally turns round*

Gwendolen, the carriage!

GWENDOLEN: Yes, mamma. (*goes out, looking back at* JACK)

LADY BRACKNELL (*sitting down*): You can take a seat, Mr Worthing. (*looks in her pocket for note-book and pencil*)

JACK: Thank you, Lady Bracknell, I prefer standing.

LADY BRACKNELL (*pencil and note-book in hand*): I feel bound to tell you that you are not down on my list of eligible young men, although I have the same list as the dear Duchess of Bolton has. We work together, in fact. However, I am quite ready to enter your name, should your answers be what a really affectionate mother requires. Do you smoke?

JACK: Well, yes, I must admit I smoke.

LADY BRACKNELL: I'm glad to hear it. A man should always have an occupation of some kind. There are far too many idle men in London as it is. How old are you?

JACK: Twenty-nine.

LADY BRACKNELL: A very good age to be married at. I have always been of opinion that a man who desires to get married should know either everything or nothing. Which do you know?

JACK (*after some hesitation*): I know nothing, Lady Bracknell.

LADY BRACKNELL: I am pleased to hear it. I do not approve of anything that tampers with natural ignorance. Ignorance is like a delicate exotic fruit; touch it and the bloom is gone. The whole theory of modern education is radically unsound. Fortunately, in England, at any rate, education produces no effect whatsoever. If it did, it would prove a serious danger to the upper classes, and probably lead to acts of violence in Grosvenor Square. What is your income?

JACK: Between seven and eight thousand a year.

LADY BRACKNELL (*makes a note in her book*): In land, or in investments?

JACK: In investments, chiefly.

LADY BRACKNELL: That is satisfactory. What between the duties expected of one during one's lifetime, and the duties exacted from one after one's death, land has ceased to be either a profit or a pleasure. It gives one position, and prevents one from keeping it up. That's all that can be said about land.

JACK: I have a country house with some land, of course, attached to it – about fifteen hundred acres, I believe; but I don't depend on that for my real income. In fact, as far as I can make out, the poachers are the only people who make anything out of it.

LADY BRACKNELL: A country house! How many bedrooms? Well, that point can be cleared up afterwards. You have a town house, I hope? A girl with a simple, unspoiled nature, like Gwendolen, could hardly be expected to reside in the country.

JACK: Well, I own a house in Belgrave Square, but it is let by the year to Lady Bloxham. Of course, I can get it back whenever I like, at six months' notice.

LADY BRACKNELL: Lady Bloxham? I don't know her.

JACK: Oh, she goes about very little. She is a lady considerably advanced in years.

LADY BRACKNELL: Ah, nowadays that is no guarantee of respectability of character. What number in Belgrave Square?

JACK: One hundrd and forty-nine.

LADY BRACKNELL (*shaking her head*): The unfashionable side. I thought there was something. However, that could easily be altered.

JACK: Do you mean the fashion, or the side?

LADY BRACKNELL (*sternly*): Both, if necessary, I presume. What are your politics?

JACK: Well, I am afraid I really have none. I am a Liberal Unionist.

LADY BRACKNELL: Oh, they count as Tories. They dine with us. Or come in the evening, at any rate. Now to minor matters. Are your parents living?

JACK: I have lost both my parents.

LADY BRACKNELL: Both? . . . That seems like carelessness. Who was your father? He was evidently a man of some wealth. Was he born in what the Radical papers call the purple of commerce, or did he rise from the ranks of the aristocracy?

JACK: I am afraid I really don't know. The fact is, Lady Bracknell, I said I had lost my parents. It would be nearer the truth to say that my parents seem to have lost me . . . I don't actually know who I am by birth. I was … well, I was found.

LADY BRACKNELL: Found!

JACK: The late Mr Thomas Cardew, an old gentleman of a very charitable and kindly disposition, found me, and gave me the name of Worthing,[4] because he happened to have a first-class ticket for Worthing in his pocket at the time. Worthing is a place in Sussex. It is a seaside resort.

LADY BRACKNELL: Where did the charitable gentleman who had a first-class ticket for this seaside resort find you?

JACK (*gravely*): In a hand-bag.

LADY BRACKNELL: A hand-bag?

JACK (*very seriously*): Yes, Lady Bracknell. I was in a hand-bag – a somewhat large, black leather hand-bag, with handles to it – an ordinary hand-bag in fact.

LADY BRACKNELL: In what locality did this Mr James, or Thomas, Cardew come across this ordinary hand-bag?

JACK: In the cloakroom at Victoria Station. It was given to him in mistake for his own.

LADY BRACKNELL: The cloakroom at Victoria Station?

JACK: Yes. The Brighton line.

LADY BRACKNELL: The line is immaterial. Mr Worthing, I confess I feel somewhat bewildered by what you have just told me. To be born, or at any rate bred, in a hand-bag, whether it had handles or not, seems to me to display a contempt for the ordinary decencies of family life that reminds one of the worst excesses of the French Revolution. And I presume you know what that unfortunate movement led to? As for the particular locality in which the hand-bag was found, a cloakroom at a railway station might serve to conceal a social indiscretion – has probably, indeed, been used for that purpose before now – but it could hardly be regarded as an assured basis for a recognised position in good society.

JACK: May I ask you then what you would advise me to do? I need hardly say I would do anything in the world to ensure Gwendolen's happiness.

LADY BRACKNELL: I would strongly advise you, Mr Worthing, to try and acquire some relations as soon as possible, and to make a definite effort to produce at any rate one parent, of either sex, before the season is quite over.

JACK: Well, I don't see how I could possibly manage to do that. I can produce the hand-bag at any moment. It is in my dressing-room at home. I really think that should satisfy you, Lady Bracknell.

LADY BRACKNELL: Me, sir! What has it to do with me? You can hardly imagine that I and Lord Bracknell would dream of allowing our only daughter – a girl brought up with the utmost care – to marry into a cloakroom, and form an alliance with a parcel. Good morning, Mr Worthing!

LADY BRACKNELL *sweeps out in majestic indignation.*

ACT TWO

*The garden at the Manor House. A flight of grey stone
steps leads up to the house. The garden, an old-fashioned
one full of roses. Time of year, July. Basket chairs, and a
table covered with books, are set under a large yew tree.*
CECILY *is at the back watering flowers.*

Enter MERRIMAN *with a card on a salver.*

MERRIMAN: Mr Ernest Worthing has just driven
over from the station. He has brought his luggage
with him.

CECILY (*takes the card and reads it*): 'Mr Ernest Worthing, B4, Albany, W'. Uncle Jack's brother! Did
you tell him Mr Worthing was in town?

MERRIMAN: Yes, miss. He seemed very much disappointed. I mentioned that you and Miss Prism
were in the garden. He said he was anxious to
speak to you privately for a moment.

CECILY: Ask Mr Ernest Worthing to come here. I
suppose you had better talk to the housekeeper
about a room for him.

MERRIMAN: Yes, miss.

MERRIMAN *goes out.*

CECILY: I have never met any really wicked person before. I feel rather frightened. I am so afraid he will look just like everyone else.

Enter ALGERNON, *very gay and debonair.*

He does!

ALGERNON (*raising his hat*): You are my little cousin Cecily, I'm sure.

CECILY: You are under some strange mistake. I am not little. In fact, I believe I am more than usually tall for my age. (ALGERNON *is rather taken aback*) But I am your cousin Cecily. You, I see from your card, are Uncle Jack's brother, my cousin Ernest, my wicked cousin Ernest.

ALGERNON: Oh! I am not really wicked at all, cousin Cecily. You mustn't think that I am wicked.

CECILY: If you are not, then you have certainly been deceiving us all in a very inexcusable manner. I hope you have not been leading a double life, pretending to be wicked and being really good all the time. That would be hyprocrisy.

ALGERNON (*looks at her in amazement*): Oh! Of course I have been rather reckless.

CECILY: I am glad to hear it.

ALGERNON: In fact, now you mention the subject, I have been very bad in my own small way.

CECILY: I don't think you should be so proud of that, though I am sure it must have been very pleasant.

ALGERNON: It is much pleasanter being here with you.

CECILY: I can't understand how you are here at all. Uncle Jack won't be back till Monday afternoon.

ALGERNON: That is a great disappointment. I am obliged to go up by the first train on Monday morning, I have a business appointment that I am anxious . . . to miss!

CECILY: Couldn't you miss it anywhere but in London?

ALGERNON: No; the appointment is in London.

CECILY: Well, I know, of course, how important it is not to keep a business engagement, if one wants to retain any sense of the beauty of life, but still I think you had better wait till Uncle Jack arrives. I know he wants to speak to you about your emigrating.

ALGERNON: About my what?

CECILY: Your emigrating. He has gone up to buy your outfit.

ALGERNON: I certainly wouldn't let Jack buy my outfit. He has no taste in neckties at all.

CECILY: I don't think you will require neckties. Uncle Jack is sending you to Australia.

ALGERNON: Australia! I'd sooner die.

CECILY: Well, he said at dinner on Wednesday night, that you would have to choose between this world, the next world, and Australia.

ALGERNON: Oh, well! The accounts I have received of Australia and the next world, are not particularly encouraging. This world is good enough for me, cousin Cecily.

CECILY: Yes, but are you good enough for it?

ALGERNON: I'm afraid I'm not that. That is why I want you to reform me. You might make that your mission, if you don't mind, cousin Cecily.

CECILY: I'm afraid I've no time, this afternoon.

ALGERNON: Well, would you mind my reforming myself this afternoon?

CECILY: It is rather Quixotic of you. But I think you should try.

ALGERNON: I will. I feel better already.

CECILY: You are looking a little worse.

ALGERNON: That is because I am hungry.

CECILY: How thoughtless of me. I should have remembered that when one is going to lead an entirely new life, one requires regular and wholesome meals. Won't you come in?

ALGERNON: Thank you. Might I have a buttonhole first? I never have any appetite unless I have a buttonhole first.

CECILY: A Maréchal Niel? (*picks up scissors*)

ALGERNON: No, I'd sooner have a pink rose.

CECILY: Why? (*cuts a flower*)

ALGERNON: Because you are like a pink rose, cousin Cecily.

CECILY: I don't think it can be right for you to talk to me like that. Miss Prism never says such things to me.

ALGERNON: Then Miss Prism is a short-sighted old lady. (CECILY *puts the rose in his buttonhole*) You are the prettiest girl I ever saw.

They pass into the house.

Enter JACK *slowly from the back of the garden. He is dressed in the deepest mourning, with crape hatband and black gloves.*

MISS PRISM: Mr Worthing!

CHASUBLE: Mr Worthing?

MISS PRISM: This is indeed a surprise. We did not look for you till Monday afternoon.

JACK (*shakes* MISS PRISM's *hand in a tragic manner*): I have returned sooner than I expected. Dr Chasuble, I hope you are well?

CHASUBLE: Dear Mr Worthing, I trust this garb of woe does not betoken some terrible calamity?

JACK: My brother.

MISS PRISM: More shameful debts and extravagance?

CHASUBLE: Still leading his life of pleasure?

JACK (*shaking his head*): Dead!

CHASUBLE: Your brother Ernest dead?

JACK: Quite dead.

MISS PRISM: What a lesson for him! I trust he will profit by it.

CHASUBLE: Mr Worthing, I offer you my sincere condolence. You have at least the consolation of knowing that you were always the most generous and forgiving of brothers.

JACK: Poor Ernest! He had many faults, but it is a sad, sad blow.

CHASUBLE: Very sad indeed. Were you with him at the end?

JACK: No. He died abroad; in Paris, in fact. I had a telegram last night from the manager of the Grand Hotel.

CHASUBLE: Was the cause of death mentioned?

JACK: A severe chill, it seems.

MISS PRISM: As a man sows, so shall he reap.

CHASUBLE (*raising his hand*): Charity, dear Miss Prism, charity! None of us are perfect. I myself am peculiarly susceptible to draughts. Will the interment take place here?

JACK: No. He seems to have expressed a desire to be buried in Paris.

CHASUBLE: In Paris! (*shakes his head*) I fear that hardly points to any very serious state of mind at the last. You would no doubt wish me to make some slight allusion to this tragic domestic affliction

next Sunday. (JACK *presses his hand convulsively*)
My sermon on the meaning of the manna in the
wilderness can be adapted to almost any occasion,
joyful, or, as in the present case, distressing. (*all
sigh*) I have preached it at harvest celebrations,
christenings, confirmations, on days of humilia-
tion and festal days. The last time I delivered it was
in the cathedral, as a charity sermon on behalf of
the Society for the Prevention of Discontent among
the Upper Orders. The bishop, who was present,
was much struck by some of the analogies I drew.

JACK: Ah! that reminds me, you mentioned christenings, I think, Dr Chasuble? I suppose you know
how to christen all right? (DR CHASUBLE *looks
astounded*) I mean, of course, you are continually
christening, aren't you?

MISS PRISM: It is, I regret to say, one of the rector's
most constant duties in this parish. I have often
spoken to the poorer classes on the subject. But
they don't seem to know what thrift is.

CHASUBLE: But is there any particular infant in
whom you are interested, Mr Worthing? Your
brother was, I believe, unmarried, was he not?

JACK: Oh yes.

MISS PRISM (*bitterly*): People who live entirely for
pleasure usually are.

JACK: But it is not for any child, dear doctor. I am
very fond of children. No! the fact is, I would like

to be christened myself, this afternoon, if you have nothing better to do.

CHASUBLE: But surely, Mr Worthing, you have been christened already?

JACK: I don't remember anything about it.

CHASUBLE: But have you any grave doubts on the subject?

JACK: I certainly intend to have. Of course I don't know if the thing would bother you in any way, or if you think I am a little too old now.

CHASUBLE: Not at all. The sprinkling, and, indeed, the immersion of adults is a perfectly canonical practice.

JACK: Immersion!

CHASUBLE: You need have no apprehensions. Sprinkling is all that is necessary, or indeed I think advisable. Our weather is so changeable. At what hour would you wish the ceremony performed?

JACK: Oh, I might trot round about five if that would suit you.

CHASUBLE: Perfectly, perfectly! In fact, I have two similar ceremonies to perform at that time. A case of twins that occurred recently in one of the outlying cottages on your own estate. Poor Jenkins the carter, a most hard-working man.

JACK: Oh! I don't see much fun in being christened along with other babies. It would be childish. Would half-past five do?

CHASUBLE: Admirably! Admirably! *(takes out watch)* And now, dear Mr Worthing, I will not intrude any longer into a house of sorrow. I would merely beg you not to be too much bowed down by grief. What seem to us bitter trials are often blessings in disguise.

MISS PRISM: This seems to me a blessing of an extremely obvious kind.

Enter CECILY *from the house.*

CECILY: Uncle Jack! Oh, I am pleased to see you back. But what horrid clothes you have got on! Do go and change them.

MISS PRISM: Cecily!

CHASUBLE: My child! my child!

CECILY *goes towards* JACK; *he kisses her brow in a melancholy manner.*

CECILY: What is the matter, Uncle Jack? Do look happy! You look as if you had toothache, and I have got such a surprise for you. Who do you think is in the dining-room? Your brother!

JACK: Who?

CECILY: Your brother Ernest. He arrived about half an hour ago.

JACK: What nonsense! I haven't got a brother.

CECILY: Oh, don't say that. However badly he may have behaved to you in the past he is still your brother. You couldn't be so heartless as to disown him. I'll tell him to come out. And you will shake hands with him, won't you, Uncle Jack? *(runs back into the house)*

CHASUBLE: These are very joyful tidings.

MISS PRISM: After we had all been resigned to his loss, his sudden return seems to me peculiarly distressing.

JACK: My brother is in the dining-room? I don't know what it all means. I think it is perfectly absurd.

Enter ALGERNON and CECILY, hand in hand. They come slowly up to JACK.

JACK: Good heavens! *(motions ALGERNON away)*

ALGERNON: Brother John, I have come down from town to tell you that I am very sorry for all the trouble I have given you, and that I intend to lead a better life in the future. *(JACK glares at him and does not take his hand)*

CECILY: Uncle Jack, you are not going to refuse your own brother's hand?

JACK: Nothing will induce me to take his hand. I think his coming down here disgraceful. He knows perfectly well why.

CECILY: Uncle Jack, do be nice. There is some good in everyone. Ernest has just been telling me about his poor invalid friend Mr Bunbury whom he goes to visit so often. And surely there must be much good in one who is kind to an invalid, and leaves the pleasures of London to sit by a bed of pain.

JACK: Oh! he has been talking about Bunbury, has he?

CECILY: Yes, he has told me all about poor Mr Bunbury, and his terrible state of health.

JACK: Bunbury! Well, I won't have him talk to you about Bunbury or about anything else. It is enough to drive one perfectly frantic.

ALGERNON: Of course I admit that the faults were all on my side. But I must say that I think that brother John's coldness to me is peculiarly painful. I expected a more enthusiastic welcome, especially considering it is the first time I have come here.

CECILY: Uncle Jack, if you don't shake hands with Ernest I will never forgive you.

JACK: Never forgive me?

CECILY: Never, never, never!

JACK: Well, this is the last time I shall ever do it. (*shakes hands with* ALGERNON *and glares*)

CHASUBLE: It's pleasant, is it not, to see so perfect a reconciliation? I think we might leave the two brothers together.

MISS PRISM: Cecily, you will come with us.

CECILY: Certainly, Miss Prism. My little task of reconciliation is over.

CHASUBLE: You have done a beautiful action today,
dear child.

MISS PRISM: We must not be premature in our
judgements.

CECILY: I feel very happy.

They all go out except JACK *and* ALGERNON.

JACK: You young scoundrel, Algy, you must get out of
this place as soon as possible. I don't allow any
Bunburying here.

Enter MERRIMAN.

MERRIMAN: I have put Mr Ernest's things in the
room next to yours, sir. I suppose that is all right?

JACK: What?

MERRIMAN: Mr Ernest's luggage, sir. I have unpacked
it and put it in the room next to your own.

JACK: His luggage?

MERRIMAN: Yes, sir. Three portmanteaus, a dressing
case, two hat-boxes, and a large luncheon-basket.

ALGERNON: I am afraid I can't stay more than a week
this time.

JACK: Merriman, order the dog-cart at once. Mr
Ernest has been suddenly called back to town.

MERRIMAN: Yes, sir. (*goes back into the house*)

ALGERNON: What a fearful liar you are, Jack. I have not been called back to town at all.

JACK: Yes, you have.

ALGERNON: I haven't heard anyone call me.

JACK: Your duty as a gentleman calls you back.

ALGERNON: My duty as a gentleman has never interfered with my pleasures in the smallest degree.

JACK: I can quite understand that.

ALGERNON: Well, Cecily is a darling.

JACK: You are not to talk of Miss Cardew like that. I don't like it.

ALGERNON: Well, I don't like your clothes. You look perfectly ridiculous in them. Why on earth don't you go up and change? It is perfectly childish to be in deep mourning for a man who is actually staying for a whole week with you in your house as a guest. I call it grotesque.

JACK: You are certainly not staying with me for a whole week as a guest or anything else. You have got to leave . . . by the four-five train.

ALGERNON: I certainly won't leave you so long as you are in mourning. It would be most unfriendly. If I were in mourning you would stay with me, I suppose. I should think it very unkind if you didn't.

JACK: Well, will you go if I change my clothes?

ALGERNON: Yes, if you are not too long. I never saw anybody take so long to dress, and with such little result.

JACK: Well, at any rate, that is better than being always over-dressed as you are.

ALGERNON: If I am occasionally a little over-dressed, I make up for it by being always immensely over-educated.

JACK: Your vanity is ridiculous, your conduct an outrage, and your presence in my garden utterly absurd. However, you have got to catch the four-five, and I hope you will have a pleasant journey back to town. This Bunburying, as you call it, has not been a great success for you. (*goes into the house*)

ALGERNON: I think it has been a great success. I'm in love with Cecily, and that is everything.

Enter CECILY *at the back of the garden. She picks up the can and begins to water the flowers.*

But I must see her before I go, and make arrangements for another Bunbury. Ah, there she is.

CECILY: Oh, I merely came back to water the roses. I thought you were with Uncle Jack.

ALGERNON: He's gone to order the dog-cart for me.

CECILY: Oh, is he going to take you for a nice drive?

ALGERNON: He's going to send me away.

CECILY: Then have we got to part?

ALGERNON: I am afraid so. It's a very painful parting.

CECILY: It is always painful to part from people whom one has known for a very brief space of time. The absence of old friends one can endure with equanimity. But even a momentary separation from anyone to whom one has just been introduced is almost unbearable.

ALGERNON: Thank you.

MERRIMAN: The dog-cart is at the door, sir.

ALGERNON *looks appealingly at* CECILY.

CECILY: It can wait, Merriman . . . for five . . . minutes.

MERRIMAN: Yes, miss.

Exit MERRIMAN.

ALGERNON: I hope, Cecily, I shall not offend you if I state quite frankly and openly that you seem to me to be in every way the visible personification of absolute perfection.

CECILY: I think your frankness does you great credit, Ernest. If you will allow me, I will copy your remarks into my diary. (*goes over to table and begins writing in diary*)

ALGERNON: Do you really keep a diary? I'd give anything to look at it. May I?

CECILY: Oh no. (*puts her hand over it*) You see, it is simply a very young girl's record of her own thoughts and impressions, and consequently meant for publication. When it appears in volume form I hope you will order a copy. But pray, Ernest, don't stop. I delight in taking down from dictation. I have reached 'absolute perfection'. You can go on. I am quite ready for more.

ALGERNON (*somewhat taken aback*): Ahem! Ahem!

CECILY: Oh, don't cough, Ernest. When one is dictating one should speak fluently and not cough. Besides, I don't know how to spell a cough. (*writes as ALGERNON speaks*)

ALGERNON (*speaking very rapidly*): Cecily, ever since I first looked upon your wonderful and incomparable beauty, I have dared to love you wildly, passionately, devotedly, hopelessly.

CECILY: I don't think that you should tell me that you love me wildly, passionately, devotedly, hopelessly. Hopelessly doesn't seem to make much sense, does it?

ALGERNON: Cecily!

Enter MERRIMAN.

MERRIMAN: The dog-cart is waiting, sir.

ALGERNON: Tell it to come round next week, at the same hour.

MERRIMAN (*looks at* CECILY, *who makes no sign*):
Yes, sir.

MERRIMAN *retires.*

CECILY: Uncle Jack would be very much annoyed if
he knew you were staying on till next week, at the
same hour.

ALGERNON: Oh, I don't care about Jack. I don't care
for anybody in the whole world but you. I love you,
Cecily. You will marry me, won't you?

CECILY: You silly boy! Of course. Why, we have been
engaged for the last three months.

ALGERNON: For the last three months?

CECILY: Yes, it will be exactly three months on
Thursday.

ALGERNON: But how did we become engaged?

CECILY: Well, ever since dear Uncle Jack first con-
fessed to us that he had a younger brother who
was very wicked and bad, you, of course, have
formed the chief topic of conversation between
myself and Miss Prism. And, of course, a man who
is much talked about is always very attractive.
One feels there must be something in him, after
all. I dare say it was foolish of me, but I fell in love
with you, Ernest.

ALGERNON: Darling. And when was the engagement
actually settled?

CECILY: On the 14th of February last. Worn out by your entire ignorance of my existence, I determined to end the matter one way or the other, and after a long struggle with myself I accepted you under this dear old tree here. The next day I bought this little ring in your name, and this is the little bangle with the true lover's knot I promised you always to wear.

ALGERNON: Did I give you this? It's very pretty, isn't it?

CECILY: Yes, you've wonderfully good taste, Ernest. It's the excuse I've always given for your leading such a bad life. And this is the box in which I keep all your dear letters. (*kneels at table, opens box, and produces letters tied up with blue ribbon*)

ALGERNON: My letters! But, my own sweet Cecily, I have never written you any letters.

CECILY: You need hardly remind me of that, Ernest. I remember only too well that I was forced to write your letters for you. I wrote always three times a week, and sometimes oftener.

ALGERNON: Oh, do let me read them, Cecily?

CECILY: Oh, I couldn't possibly. They would make you far too conceited. (*replaces box*) The three you wrote me after I had broken off the engagement are so beautiful, and so badly spelled, that even now I can hardly read them without crying a little.

ALGERNON: But was our engagement ever broken off?

CECILY: Of course it was. On the 22nd of last March. You can see the entry if you like. (*shows diary*) 'Today I broke off my engagement with Ernest. I feel it is better to do so. The weather still continues charming.'

ALGERNON: But why on earth did you break it off? What had I done? I had done nothing at all. Cecily, I am very much hurt indeed to hear you broke it off. Particularly when the weather was so charming.

CECILY: It would hardly have been a really serious engagement if it hadn't been broken off at least once. But I forgave you before the week was out.

ALGERNON (*crossing to her and kneeling*): What a perfect angel you are, Cecily.

CECILY: You dear romantic boy. (*he kisses her, she puts her fingers through his hair*) I hope your hair curls naturally, does it?

ALGERNON: Yes, darling, with a little help from others.

CECILY: I am so glad.

ALGERNON: You'll never break off our engagement again, Cecily?

CECILY: I don't think I could break it off now that I have actually met you. Besides, of course, there is the question of your name.

ALGERNON: Yes, of course. (*nervously*)

CECILY: You must not laugh at me, darling, but it had always been a girlish dream of mine to love someone whose name was Ernest.

ALGERNON *rises*, CECILY *also*.

There is something in that name that seems to inspire absolute confidence. I pity any poor married woman whose husband is not called Ernest.

ALGERNON: But, my dear child, do you mean to say you could not love me if I had some other name?

CECILY: But what name?

ALGERNON: Oh, any name you like – Algernon – for instance . . .

CECILY: But I don't like the name of Algernon.

ALGERNON: Well, my own dear, sweet, loving little darling, I really can't see why you should object to the name of Algernon. It is not at all a bad name. In fact, it is rather an aristocratic name. Half of the chaps who get into the bankruptcy court are called Algernon. But seriously, Cecily – (*moving to her*) – if my name was Algy, couldn't you love me?

CECILY (*rising*): I might respect you, Ernest, I might admire your character, but I fear that I should not be able to give you my undivided attention.

ALGERNON: Ahem! Cecily! (*picking up hat*) Your rector here is, I suppose, thoroughly experienced in the practice of all the rites and ceremonials of the church?

CECILY: Oh, yes. Dr Chasuble is a most learned man. He has never written a single book, so you can imagine how much he knows.

ALGERNON: I must see him at once on a most important christening – I mean on most important business.

CECILY: Oh!

ALGERNON: I shan't be away more than half an hour.

CECILY: Considering that we have been engaged since February the 14th, and that I only met you today for the first time, I think it is rather hard that you should leave me for so long a period as half an hour. Couldn't you make it twenty minutes?

ALGERNON: I'll be back in no time. (*kisses her and rushes down the garden*)

CECILY: What an impetuous boy he is! I like his hair so much. I must enter his proposal in my diary.

Enter MERRIMAN.

MERRIMAN: A Miss Fairfax has just called to see Mr Worthing. On very important business, Miss Fairfax states.

CECILY: Isn't Mr Worthing in his library?

MERRIMAN: Mr Worthing went over in the direction of the rectory some time ago.

CECILY: Pray ask the lady to come out here; Mr Worthing is sure to be back soon. And you can bring tea.

MERRIMAN: Yes, miss. (*goes out*)

CECILY: Miss Fairfax! I suppose one of the many good elderly women who are associated with Uncle Jack in some of his philanthropic work in London. I don't quite like women who are interested in philanthropic work. I think it is so forward of them.

Enter MERRIMAN.

MERRIMAN: Miss Fairfax.

Enter GWENDOLEN. *Exit* MERRIMAN.

CECILY (*advancing to meet her*): Pray let me introduce myself to you. My name is Cecily Cardew.

GWENDOLEN: Cecily Cardew? (*moving to her and shaking hands*) What a very sweet name! Something tells me that we are going to be great friends. I like you already more than I can say. My first impressions of people are never wrong.

CECILY: How nice of you to like me so much after we have known each other such a comparatively short time. Pray sit down.

GWENDOLEN (*still standing up*): I may call you Cecily, may I not?

CECILY: With pleasure!

GWENDOLEN: And you will always call me Gwendolen, won't you?

CECILY: If you wish.

GWENDOLEN: Then that is all quite settled, is it not?

CECILY: I hope so.

A pause. They both sit down together.

GWENDOLEN: Perhaps this might be a favourable opportunity for my mentioning who I am. My father is Lord Bracknell. You have never heard of papa, I suppose?

CECILY: I don't think so.

GWENDOLEN: Outside the family circle, papa, I am glad to say, is entirely unknown. I think that is quite as it should be. The home seems to me to be the proper sphere for the man. And certainly once a man begins to neglect his domestic duties he becomes painfully effeminate, does he not? And I don't like that. It makes men so very attractive. Cecily, mamma, whose views on education are remarkably strict, has brought me up to be extremely short-sighted; it is part of her system; so do you mind my looking at you through my glasses?

CECILY: Oh! not at all, Gwendolen. I am very fond of being looked at.

GWENDOLEN (*after examining* CECILY *carefully through a lorgnette*): You are here on a short visit, I suppose.

CECILY: Oh no! I live here.

GWENDOLEN (*severely*): Really? Your mother, no doubt, or some female relative of advanced years, resides here also?

CECILY: Oh no! I have no mother, nor, in fact, any relations.

GWENDOLEN Indeed?

CECILY: My dear guardian, with the assistance of Miss Prism, has the arduous task of looking after me.

GWENDOLEN: Your guardian?

CECILY: Yes, I am Mr Worthing's ward.

GWENDOLEN: Oh! It is strange he never mentioned to me that he had a ward. How secretive of him! He grows more interesting hourly. I am not sure, however, that the news inspires me with feelings of unmixed delight. (*rising and going to her*) I am very fond of you, Cecily; I have liked you ever since I met you! But I am bound to state that now that I know that you are Mr Worthing's ward, I cannot help expressing a wish you were – well, just a little older than you seem to be – and not quite so very alluring in appearance. In fact, if I may speak candidly –

CECILY: Pray do! I think that whenever one has anything unpleasant to say, one should always be quite candid.

GWENDOLEN: Well, to speak with perfect candour, Cecily, I wish that you were fully forty-two, and more than usually plain for your age. Ernest has a strong upright nature. He is the very soul of truth and honour. Disloyalty would be as impossible to him as deception. But even men of the noblest possible moral character are extremely susceptible to the influence of the physical charms of others. Modern no less than ancient history supplies us with many most painful examples of what I refer to. If it were not so, indeed, history would be quite unreadable.

CECILY: I beg your pardon, Gwendolen, did you say Ernest?

GWENDOLEN: Yes.

CECILY: Oh, but it is not Mr Ernest Worthing who is my guardian. It is his brother – his elder brother.

GWENDOLEN (*sitting down again*): Ernest never mentioned to me that he had a brother.

CECILY: I am sorry to say they have not been on good terms for a long time.

GWENDOLEN: Ah! that accounts for it. And now that I think of it I have never heard any man mention his brother. The subject seems distasteful to most men. Cecily, you have lifted a load from my mind.

I was growing almost anxious. It would have been terrible if any cloud had come across a friendship like ours would it not? Of course you are quite, quite sure that it is not Mr Ernest Worthing who is your guardian?

CECILY: Quite sure. (*a pause*) In fact, I am going to be his.

GWENDOLEN (*enquiringly*): I beg your pardon?

CECILY (*rather shy and confidingly*): Dearest Gwendolen, there is no reason why I should make a secret of it to you. Our little county newspaper is sure to chronicle the fact next week. Mr Ernest Worthing and I are engaged to be married.

GWENDOLEN (*quite politely, rising*): My darling Cecily, I think there must be some slight error. Mr Ernest Worthing is engaged to me. The announcement will appear in the *Morning Post* on Saturday at the latest.

CECILY (*very politely, rising*): I am afraid you must be under some misconception. Ernest proposed to me exactly ten minutes ago. (*shows diary*)

GWENDOLEN (*examines diary through her lorgnette carefully*): It is certainly very curious, for he asked me to be his wife yesterday afternoon at 5.30. If you would care to verify the incident, pray do so. (*produces diary of her own*) I never travel without my diary. One should always have something sensational to read in the train. I am so sorry, dear

Cecily, if it is any disappointment to you, but I am afraid I have the prior claim.

CECILY: It would distress me more than I can tell you, dear Gwendolen, if it caused you any mental or physical anguish, but I feel bound to point out that since Ernest proposed to you he clearly has changed his mind.

GWENDOLEN (*meditatively*): If the poor fellow has been entrapped into any foolish promise I shall consider it my duty to rescue him at once, and with a firm hand.

CECILY (*thoughtfully and sadly*): Whatever unfortunate entanglement my dear boy may have got into, I will never reproach him with it after we are married.

GWENDOLEN: Do you allude to me, Miss Cardew, as an entanglement? You are presumptuous. On an occasion of this kind it becomes more than a moral duty to speak one's mind. It becomes a pleasure.

CECILY: Do you suggest, Miss Fairfax, that I entrapped Ernest into an engagement? How dare you? This is no time for wearing the shallow mask of manners. When I see a spade I call it a spade.

GWENDOLEN (*satirically*): I am glad to say that I have never seen a spade. It is obvious that our social spheres have been widely different.

Enter JACK.

GWENDOLEN (*catching sight of him*): Ernest! My own Ernest!

JACK: Gwendolen! Darling! (*offers to kiss her*)

GWENDOLEN (*drawing back*): A moment! May I ask if you are engaged to be married to this young lady? (*points to* CECILY)

JACK (*laughing*): To dear little Cecily! Of course not! What could have put such an idea into your pretty little head?

GWENDOLEN: Thank you. You may! (*offers her cheek*)

CECILY (*very sweetly*): I knew there must be some misunderstanding, Miss Fairfax. The gentleman whose arm is at present round your waist is my guardian, Mr John Worthing.

GWENDOLEN: I beg your pardon?

CECILY: This is Uncle Jack.

GWENDOLEN (*receding*): Jack! Oh!

Enter ALGERNON.

CECILY: Here is Ernest.

ALGERNON (*goes straight over to* CECILY *without noticing anyone else*): My own love! (*offers to kiss her*)

CECILY (*drawing back*): A moment, Ernest! May I ask you – are you engaged to be married to this young lady?

ALGERNON (*looking round*): To what young lady? Good heavens! Gwendolen!

CECILY: Yes! to good heavens, Gwendolen, I mean to Gwendolen.

ALGERNON (*laughing*): Of course not! What could have put such an idea into your pretty little head?

CECILY: Thank you. (*presenting her cheek to be kissed*) You may. (ALGERNON *kisses her*)

GWENDOLEN: I felt there was some slight error, Miss Cardew. The gentleman who is now embracing you is my cousin, Mr Algernon Moncrieff.

CECILY (*breaking away from* ALGERNON): Algernon Moncrieff! Oh!

The two girls move towards each other and put their arms round each other's waists as if for protection.

CECILY: Are you called Algernon?

ALGERNON: I cannot deny it.

CECILY: Oh!

GWENDOLEN: Is your name really John?

JACK (*standing rather proudly*): I could deny it if I liked. I could deny anything if I liked. But my name certainly is John. It has been John for years.

CECILY (*to* GWENDOLEN): A gross deception has been practised on both of us.

GWENDOLEN: My poor wounded Cecily!

CECILY: My sweet wronged Gwendolen!

GWENDOLEN (*slowly and seriously*): You will call me sister, will you not?

They embrace, JACK *and* ALGERNON *groan and walk up and down.*

CECILY (*rather brightly*): There is just one question I would like to be allowed to ask my guardian.

GWENDOLEN: An admirable idea! Mr Worthing, there is just one question I would like to be permitted to put to you. Where is your brother Ernest? We are both engaged to be married to your brother Ernest, so it is a matter of some importance to us to know where your brother Ernest is at present.

JACK (*slowly and hesitatingly*): Gwendolen – Cecily – it is very painful for me to be forced to speak the truth. It is the first time in my life that I have ever been reduced to such a painful position, and I am really quite inexperienced in doing anything of the kind. However, I will tell you quite frankly that I have no brother Ernest. I have no brother at all. I never had a brother in my life, and I certainly have not the smallest intention of ever having one in the future.

CECILY (*surprised*): No brother at all?

JACK (*cheerily*): None!

GWENDOLEN (*severely*): Had you never a brother of any kind?

JACK (*pleasantly*): Never. Not even of any kind.

GWENDOLEN: I am afraid it is quite clear, Cecily, that neither of us is engaged to be married to anyone.

CECILY: It is not a very pleasant position for a young girl suddenly to find herself in. Is it?

GWENDOLEN: Let us go into the house. They will hardly venture to come after us there.

CECILY: No, men are so cowardly, aren't they?

They retire into the house with scornful looks.

JACK: This ghastly state of things is what you call Bunburying, I suppose?

ALGERNON: Yes, and a perfectly wonderful Bunbury it is. The most wonderful Bunbury I have ever had in my life.

JACK: Well, you've no right whatsoever to Bunbury here.

ALGERNON: That is absurd. One has a right to Bunbury anywhere one chooses. Every serious Bunburyist knows that.

JACK: Serious Bunburyist! Good heavens!

ALGERNON: Well, one must be serious about something, if one wants to have any amusement in life. I happen to be serious about Bunburying. What on earth you are serious about I haven't got the remotest idea. About everything, I should fancy. You have such an absolutely trivial nature.

JACK: Well, the only small satisfaction I have in the whole of this wretched business is that your friend Bunbury is quite exploded. You won't be able to run down to the country quite so often as you used to do, dear Algy. And a very good thing too.

ALGERNON: Your brother is a little off colour, isn't he, dear Jack? You won't be able to disappear to London quite so frequently as your wicked custom was. And not a bad thing either.

2

The Decay of Lying
An Observation

A dialogue.
Persons: *Cyril and Vivian*.
Scene: *the library of a country house in Nottinghamshire*.

CYRIL *(coming in through the open window from the terrace)*: My dear Vivian, don't coop yourself up all day in the library. It is a perfectly lovely afternoon. The air is exquisite. There is a mist upon the woods, like the purple bloom upon a plum. Let us go and lie on the grass and smoke cigarettes and enjoy Nature.

VIVIAN: Enjoy Nature! I am glad to say that I have entirely lost that faculty. People tell us that Art makes us love Nature more than we loved her before; that it reveals her secrets to us; and that after a careful study of Corot and Constable we see things in her that had escaped our observation. My own experience is that the more we study Art, the less we care for Nature. What Art really reveals to us is Nature's lack of design, her curious crudities, her extraordinary monotony, her absolutely unfinished condition. Nature has good intentions, of course, but, as Aristotle once said, she cannot carry them out. When I look at a landscape I cannot help seeing all its defects. It is fortunate for us, however, that Nature is so imperfect, as otherwise we should have had no art at all. Art is our spirited protest, our gallant attempt to teach Nature her proper place. As for the infinite variety of Nature, that is a pure myth. It is not to be found in Nature herself. It resides in the imagination, or fancy, or cultivated blindness of the man who looks at her.

CYRIL: Well, you need not look at the landscape. You can lie on the grass and smoke and talk.

VIVIAN: But Nature is so uncomfortable. Grass is hard and lumpy and damp, and full of dreadful black insects. Why, even Morris's poorest workman could make you a more comfortable seat than the whole of Nature can. Nature pales before the furniture of 'the street which from Oxford has borrowed its name', as the poet you love so much once vilely phrased it. I don't complain. If Nature had been comfortable, mankind would never have invented architecture, and I prefer houses to the open air. In a house we all feel of the proper proportions. Everything is subordinated to us, fashioned for our use and our pleasure. Egotism itself, which is so necessary to a proper sense of human dignity, is entirely the result of indoor life. Out of doors one becomes abstract and impersonal. One's individuality absolutely leaves one. And then Nature is so indifferent, so unappreciative. Whenever I am walking in the park here, I always feel that I am no more to her than the cattle that browse on the slope, or the burdock that blooms in the ditch. Nothing is more evident than that Nature hates Mind. Thinking is the most unhealthy thing in the world, and people die of it just as they die of any other disease. Fortunately, in England at any rate, thought is not catching. Our splendid physique as a people is entirely due to our national stupidity. I only hope we shall be able to keep this great historic bulwark of our happiness for many years to come; but I am afraid that we are beginning to be over-educated; at least everybody who is incapable of learning has taken to teaching – that is really what our enthusiasm for education has come to. In the meantime, you had better go back to your wearisome uncomfortable Nature, and leave me to correct my proofs.

CYRIL: Writing an article! That is not very consistent after what you have just said.

VIVIAN: Who wants to be consistent? The dullard and the doctrinaire, the tedious people who carry out their principles to the bitter end of action, to the *reductio ad absurdum* of practice. Not I. Like Emerson, I write over the door of my library the word 'Whim'. Besides, my article is really a most salutary and valuable warning. If it is attended to, there may be a new Renaissance of Art.

CYRIL: What is the subject?

VIVIAN: I intend to call it 'The Decay of Lying: A Protest'.

CYRIL: Lying! I should have thought that our politicians kept up that habit.

VIVIAN: I assure you that they do not. They never rise beyond the level of misrepresentation, and actually condescend to prove, to discuss, to argue. How different from the temper of the true liar, with his frank, fearless statements, his superb responsibility, his healthy, natural disdain of proof of any kind! After all, what is a fine lie? Simply that which is its own evidence. If a man is sufficiently unimaginative to produce evidence in support of a lie, he might just as well speak the truth at once. No, the politicians won't do. Something may, perhaps, be urged on behalf of the Bar. The mantle of the Sophist has fallen on its members. Their feigned ardours and unreal rhetoric are delightful. They can make the worse appear the better cause, as though they were fresh from Leontine schools, and have been known to wrest from reluctant juries triumphant verdicts of acquittal for their clients, even when those clients, as often happens, were clearly and unmistakeably innocent. But they are briefed by the prosaic, and are not ashamed to appeal to precedent. In spite of their endeavours, the truth will out. Newspapers, even, have degenerated. They may now be absolutely relied upon. One feels it as one wades through their columns. It is always the unreadable that occurs. I am afraid that there is not much to be said in favour of either the lawyer or the journalist. Besides what I am pleading for is Lying in art. Shall I read you what I have written? It might do you a great deal of good.

CYRIL: Certainly, if you give me a cigarette. Thanks. By the way, what magazine do you intend it for?

VIVIAN: For the *Retrospective Review*. I think I told you that the elect had revived it.

CYRIL: Whom do you mean by 'the elect'?

VIVIAN: Oh, The Tired Hedonists of course. It is a club to which I belong. We are supposed to wear faded roses in our button-holes when we meet, and to have a sort of cult for Domitian. I am afraid you are not eligible. You are too fond of simple pleasures.

CYRIL: I should be blackballed on the ground of animal spirits, I suppose?

VIVIAN: Probably. Besides, you are little too old. We don't admit anybody who is of the usual age.

CYRIL: Well, I should fancy you are all a good deal bored with each other.

VIVIAN: We are. That is one of the objects of the club. Now, if you promise not to interrupt too often, I will read you my article.

CYRIL: You will find me all attention.

VIVIAN (reading in a very clear, musical voice): 'THE DECAY OF LYING: A PROTEST. – One of the chief causes that can be assigned for the curiously commonplace character of most of the literature of our age is undoubtedly the decay of Lying as an art, a science and a social pleasure. The ancient historians gave us delightful fiction in the form of fact; the modern novelist presents us with dull facts under the guise of fiction. The Blue-Book is rapidly becoming his ideal both for method and manner. He has his tedious *document humain*, his miserable little *coin de la creation*, into which he peers with his microscope. He is to be found at the Librairie Nationale, or at the British Museum, shamelessly reading up his subject. He has not even the courage of other people's ideas, but insists on going directly to life for everything, and ultimately, between encyclopaedias and personal experience, he comes to the ground, having drawn his types from the family circle or from the weekly washerwoman, and having acquired an amount of useful information from which never, even in his most meditative moments, can he thoroughly free himself.

'The loss that results to literature in general from this false ideal of our time can hardly be overestimated. People have a careless way of talking about a 'born liar', just as they talk about a 'born poet'. But in both cases they are wrong. Lying and poetry are arts – arts, as Plato saw, not unconnected with each other – and they require the most careful study, the most disinterested devotion. Indeed, they have their technique, just as the more material arts of painting and sculpture have their subtle secrets of form and colour, their craft-mysteries, their deliberate artistic methods. As one knows the poet by his fine music, so one can recognize the liar by his rich rhythmic utterance, and in neither case will the casual inspiration of the moment suffice. Here, as elsewhere, practice must precede perfection. But in modern days while the fashion of writing poetry has become far too common, and should, if possible, be discouraged, the fashion of lying has almost fallen into disrepute. Many a young man starts in life with a natural gift for exaggeration which, if nurtured in congenial and sympathetic surroundings, or by the imitation of the best models, might grow into something really great and wonderful. But, as a rule, he comes to nothing. He either falls into careless habits of accuracy—'

CYRIL: My dear fellow!

VIVIAN: Please don't interrupt in the middle of a sentence. 'He either falls into careless habits of accuracy, or takes to frequenting the society of the aged and the well-informed. Both things are equally fatal to his imagination, as indeed they would be fatal to the imagination of anybody, and in a short time he develops a morbid and unhealthy faculty of truth-telling, begins to verify all statements made in his presence, has no hesitation in contradicting people who are much younger than himself, and often ends by writing novels which are so lifelike that no one can possibly believe in their probability. This is no isolated instance that we are giving. It is simply one example out of many; and if something cannot be done to check, or at least to modify, our monstrous worship of facts, Art will become sterile, and beauty will pass away from the land' . . . The public imagine that, because they are interested in their immediate surroundings, Art should be interested in them also, and should take them as her subject-matter. But the mere fact that they are interested in these things makes them unsuitable subjects for Art. The only beautiful things, as somebody once said, are the things that do not concern us. As long as a thing is useful or necessary to us, or affects us in any way, either for pain or for pleasure, or appeals strongly to our sympathies, or is a vital part of the environment in which we live, it is outside the proper sphere of art. To art's subject-matter we should be more or less indifferent. We should, at any rate, have no preferences, no prejudices, no partisan feeling of any kind. It is exactly because Hecuba is nothing to us that her sorrows are such an admirable motive for a tragedy. I do not know anything in the whole history of literature sadder than the artistic career of Charles Reade. He wrote one beautiful book, *The Cloister and the Hearth*, a book as much above *Romola* as *Romola* is above *Daniel Deronda*, and wasted the rest of his life in a foolish attempt to be modern, to draw public attention to the state of our convict prisons, and the management of our private lunatic asylums. Charles Dickens was depressing enough in all conscience when he tried to arouse our sympathy for the victims of the poor-law administration; but Charles Reade, an artist, a scholar, a man with a true sense of beauty, raging and roaring over the abuses of contemporary life like a common pamphleteer or a sensational journalist, is really a sight for the angels to weep over. Believe me, my dear Cyril, modernity of form and modernity of subject-matter are entirely and absolutely wrong. We have mistaken the common livery of the age for the vesture of the Muses and spend our days in the sordid streets and hideous suburbs of our vile cities when we should be out on the hillside with Apollo. Certainly we are a degraded race, and have sold our birthright for a mess of facts.

CYRIL: There is something in what you say, and there is no doubt that whatever amusement we may find in reading a purely modern novel, we have rarely any artistic pleasure in re-reading it. And this is perhaps the best rough test of what is literature and what is not. If one cannot enjoy reading a book over and over again, there is no use reading it at all. But what do you say about the return to Life and Nature? This is the panacea that is always being recommended to us.

VIVIAN: I will read you what I say on that subject. The passage comes later on in the article, but I may as well give it to you now:

'The popular cry of our time is "Let us return to Life and Nature; they will recreate Art for us, and send the red blood coursing through her veins; they will shoe her feet with swiftness and make her hand strong." But, alas! we are mistaken in our amiable and well-meaning efforts. Nature is always behind the age. And as for Life, she is the solvent that breaks up Art, the enemy that lays waste her house.'

CYRIL: What do you mean by saying that Nature is always behind the age?

VIVIAN: Well, perhaps that is rather cryptic. What I mean is this. If we take Nature to mean natural simple instinct as opposed to self-conscious culture, the work produced under this influence is always old-fashioned, antiquated, and out of date. One touch of Nature may make the whole world kin, but two touches of Nature will destroy any work of Art. If, on the other hand, we regard Nature as the collection of phenomena external to man, people only discover in her what they bring to her. She has no suggestions of her own. Wordsworth went to the lakes, but he was never a lake poet. He found in stones the sermons he had already hidden there. He went moralizing about the district, but his good work was produced when he returned, not to Nature but to poetry. Poetry gave him 'Laodamia', and the fine sonnets, and the great Ode, such as it is. Nature gave him 'Martha Ray' and 'Peter Bell', and the address to Mr Wilkinson's spade.

CYRIL: I think that view might be questioned. I am rather inclined to believe in 'the impulse from a

vernal wood', though of course the artistic value
of such an impulse depends entirely on the kind of
temperament that receives it, so that the return to
Nature would come to mean simply the advance
to a great personality. You would agree with that,
I fancy. However, proceed with your article.

VIVIAN (*reading*): 'Art begins with abstract decor-
ation with purely imaginative and pleasurable work
dealing with what is unreal and non-existent. This
is the first stage. Then Life becomes fascinated
with this new wonder, and asks to be admitted into
the charmed circle. Art takes life as part of her
rough material, recreates it, and refashions it in
fresh forms, is absolutely indifferent to fact, invents,
imagines, dreams, and keeps between herself and
reality the impenetrable barrier of beautiful style,
of decorative or ideal treatment. The third stage is
when Life gets the upper hand, and drives Art out
into the wilderness. This is the true decadence, and
it is from this that we are now suffering.'

And now let me read you a passage which seems
to me to settle the question very completely.

'It was not always thus. We need not say anything about the poets, for they, with the unfortunate exception of Mr Wordsworth, have been
really faithful to their high mission, and are
universally recognized as being absolutely
unreliable. But in the works of Herodotus, who,

in spite of the shallow and ungenerous attempts of modern sciolists to verify his history, may justly be called the 'Father of Lies'; in the published speeches of Cicero and the biographies of Suetonius; in Tacitus at his best; in Pliny's *Natural History*; in Hanno's *Periplus*; in all the early chronicles; in the Lives of the Saints; in Froissart and Sir Thomas Mallory; in the travels of Marco Polo; in Olaus Magnus, and Aldrovandus, and Conrad Lycosthenes, with his magnificent *Prodigiorum et Ostentorum Chronicon*; in the autobiography of Benvenuto Cellini; in the memoirs of Casanuova; in Defoe's *History of the Plague*; in Boswell's *Life of Johnson*; in Napoleon's despatches, and in the works of our own Carlyle, whose *French Revolution* is one of the most fascinating historical novels ever written, facts are either kept in their proper subordinate position, or else entirely excluded on the general ground of dulness. Now, everything is changed. Facts are not merely finding a footing-place in history, but they are usurping the domain of Fancy, and have invaded the kingdom of Romance. Their chilling touch is over everything. They are vulgarizing mankind. The crude commercialism of America, its materializing spirit, its indifference to the poetical side of things, and its lack of imagination and of high

unattainable ideals, are entirely due to that country having adopted for its national hero a man,
who according to his own confession, was incapable of telling a lie, and it is not too much to say
that the story of George Washington and the
cherry-tree has done more harm, and in a shorter
space of time, than any other moral tale in the
whole of literature.'

CYRIL: My dear boy!

VIVIAN: I assure you it is the case, and the amusing
part of the whole thing is that the story of the
cherry-tree is an absolute myth. However, you
must not think that I am too despondent about
the artistic future either of America or of our own
country. Listen to this:

'That some change will take place before this
century has drawn to its close we have no doubt
whatsoever. Bored by the tedious and improv-
ing conversation of those who have neither the
wit to exaggerate nor the genius to romance, tired
of the intelligent person whose reminiscences are
always based upon memory, whose statements are
invariably limited by probability, and who is at any
time liable to be corroborated by the merest Phil-
istine who happens to be present, Society sooner
or later must return to its lost leader, the cultured
and fascinating liar. Who he was who first, without ever having gone out to the rude chase, told the

wondering cavemen at sunset how he had dragged the Megatherium from the purple darkness of its jasper cave, or slain the Mammoth in single combat and brought back its gilded tusks, we cannot tell, and not one of our modern anthropologists, for all their much-boasted science, has had the ordinary courage to tell us. Whatever was his name or race, he certainly was the true founder of social inter-course. For the aim of the liar is simply to charm, to delight, to give pleasure. He is the very basis of civ-ilized society, and without him a dinner party, even at the mansions of the great, is as dull as a lecture at the Royal Society, or a debate at the Incorporated Authors, or one of Mr Burnand's far-cical comedies.

'Nor will he be welcomed by society alone. Art, breaking from the prison-house of realism, will run to greet him, and will kiss his false, beautiful lips, knowing that he alone is in possession of the great secret of all her manifestations, the secret that Truth is entirely and absolutely a matter of style; while Life – poor, probable, uninteresting human life – tired of repeating herself for the benefit of Mr Herbert Spencer, scientific histor-ians, and the compilers of statistics in general, will follow meekly after him, and try to reproduce, in her own simple and untutored way, some of the marvels of which he talks.

'No doubt there will always be critics who, like a certain writer in the *Saturday Review*, will gravely censure the teller of fairy tales for his defective knowledge of natural history, who will measure imaginative work by their own lack of any imaginative faculty, and will hold up their ink-stained hands in horror if some honest gentleman, who has never been farther than the yew-trees of his own garden, pens a fascinating book of travels like Sir John Mandeville, or, like great Raleigh, writes a whole history of the world, without knowing anything whatsoever about the past. To excuse themselves they will try and shelter under the shield of him who made Prospero the magician, and gave him Caliban and Ariel as his servants, who heard the Tritons blowing their horns round the coral reefs of the Enchanted Isle, and the fairies singing to each other in a wood near Athens, who led the phantom kings in dim procession across the misty Scottish heath, and hid Hecate in a cave with the weird sister. They will call upon Shakespeare – they always do – and will quote that hackneyed passage about Art holding the mirror up to Nature, forgetting that this unfortunate aphorism is deliberately said by Hamlet in order to convince the bystanders of his absolute insanity in all art-matters.'

CYRIL: Ahem! Another cigarette, please.

VIVIAN: My dear fellow, whatever you may say, it is merely a dramatic utterance, and no more represents Shakespeare's real views upon art than the speeches of Iago represent his real views upon morals. But let me get to the end of the passage:

'Art finds her own perfection within, and not outside of, herself. She is not to be judged by any external standard of resemblance. She is a veil, rather than a mirror. She has flowers that no forests know of, birds that no woodland possesses. She makes and unmakes many worlds, and can draw the moon from heaven with a scarlet thread. Hers are the "forms more real than living man", and hers the great archetypes of which things that have existence are but unfinished copies. Nature has, in her eyes, no laws, no uniformity. She can work miracles at her will, and when she calls monsters from the deep they come. She can bid the almond tree blossom in winter, and send the snow upon the ripe cornfield. At her word the frost lays its silver finger on the burning mouth of June, and the winged lions creep out from the hollows of the Lydian hills. The dryads peer from the thicket as she passes by, and the brown fauns smile strangely at her when she comes near them. She has hawk-faced gods that worship her, and the centaurs gallop at her side.'

CYRIL: I like that. I can see it. Is that the end?

VIVIAN: No. There is one more passage, but it is purely practical. It simply suggests some methods by which we could revive this lost art of Lying.

CYRIL: Well, before you read it to me, I should like to ask you a question. What do you mean by saying that life, 'poor, probable, uninteresting human life', will try to reproduce the marvels of art? I can quite understand your objection to art being treated as a mirror. You think it would reduce genius to the position of a cracked looking glass. But you don't mean to say that you seriously believe that Life imitates Art, that Life in fact is the mirror, and Art the reality?

VIVIAN: Certainly I do. Paradox though it may seem – and paradoxes are always dangerous things – it is none the less true that Life imitates art far more than Art imitates life . . . In the year 1879, just after I had left Oxford, I met at a reception at the house of one of the Foreign Ministers a woman of very curious exotic beauty. We became great friends, and were constantly together. And yet what interested most in her was not her beauty, but her character, her entire vagueness of character. She seemed to have no personality at all, but simply the possibility of many types. Sometimes she would give herself up entirely to art, turn her drawing-room into a studio, and spend two or three days a week at picture galleries or museums. Then she would take to attending race-meetings, wear the most horsey clothes, and talk about nothing but betting. She abandoned religion for mesmerism, mesmerism for politics, and politics for thematic excitements of philanthropy. In fact, she was a kind of Proteus, and as much a failure in all her transformations as was that wondrous sea-god when Odysseus laid hold of him. One day a serial began in one of the French magazines. At that time I used to read serial stories, and I well remember the shock of surprise I felt when I came to the description of the heroine. She was so like my friend that I brought her the magazine, and she recognized herself in it immediately, and seemed fascinated by the resemblance. I should tell you, by the way, that the story was translated from some dead Russian writer, so that the author had not taken his type from my friend. Well, to put the matter briefly, some months afterwards I was in Venice, and finding the magazine in the reading-room of the hotel, I took it up casually to see what had become of the heroine. It was a most piteous tale, as the girl had ended by running away with a man absolutely inferior to her, not merely in social station, but in character and intellect also. I wrote to my friend that evening about my views on John Bellini, and the admirable ices at Florio's, and the artistic value of gondolas, but added a postscript to the effect that her double in the story had behaved in a very silly manner. I don't know why I added that, but I remember I had a sort of dread over me that she might do the same thing. Before my letter had reached her, she had run away with a man who deserted her in six months. I saw her in 1884 in Paris, where she was living with her mother, and I asked her whether the story had had anything to do with her action. She told me that she had felt an absolutely irresistible impulse to follow the heroine step by step in her strange and fatal progress, and that it was with a feeling of real terror that she had looked forward to the last few chapters of the story. When they appeared, it seemed to her that she was compelled to reproduce them in life, and she did so. It was a most clear example of this imitative instinct of which I was speaking, and an extremely tragic one.

However, I do not wish to dwell any further upon individual instances. Personal experience is a most vicious and limited circle. All that I desire to point out is the general principle that Life imitates Art far more than Art imitates Life, and I feel sure that if you think seriously about it you will find that it is true. Life holds the mirror up to Art, and either reproduces some strange type imagined by painter or sculptor, or realizes in fact what has been dreamed in fiction. Scientifically speaking, the basis of life – the energy of life, as Aristotle would call it – is simply the desire for expression, and Art is always presenting various forms through which this expression can be attained. Life seizes on them and uses them, even if they be to her own hurt. Young men have committed suicide because Rolla did so, have died by their own hand because by his own hand Werther died. Think of what we owe to the imitation of Christ, of what we owe to the imitation of Caesar.

CYRIL: The theory is certainly a very curious one, but to make it complete you must show that Nature, no less than Life, is an imitation of Art. Are you prepared to prove that?

VIVIAN: My dear fellow, I am prepared to prove anything.

CYRIL: Nature follows the landscape painter then, and takes her effects from him?

VIVIAN: Certainly. Where, if not from the Impressionists, do we get those wonderful brown fogs that come creeping down our streets, blurring the gas-lamps and changing the houses into monstrous shadows? To whom, if not to them and their master, do we owe the lovely silver mists that brood over our river, and turn to faint forms of fading grace curved bridge and swaying barge? The extraordinary change that has taken place in the climate of London during the last ten years is entirely due to this particular school of Art. You smile. Consider the matter from a scientific or a metaphysical point of view, and you will find that I am right. For what is Nature? Nature is no great mother who has borne us. She is our creation. It is in our brain that she quickens to life. Things are because we see them, and what we see, and how we see it, depends on the Arts that have influenced us. To look at a thing is very different from seeing a thing. One does not see anything until one sees its beauty. Then, and then only, does it come into existence. At present, people see fogs, not because there are fogs, but because poets and painters have taught them the mysterious loveliness of such effects. There may have been fogs for centuries in London. I dare say there were. But no one saw them, and so we do not know anything about them. They did not exist till Art had invented them. Now, it must be admitted, fogs are carried to excess. They have become the mere mannerism of a clique, and the exaggerated realism of their method gives dull people bronchitis. Where the cultured catch an effect, the uncultured catch cold. And so, let us be humane, and invite Art to turn her wonderful eyes elsewhere. She has done so already, indeed. That white quivering sunlight that one sees now in France, with its strange blotches of mauve, and its restless violet shadows, is her latest fancy, and, on the whole, Nature reproduces it quite admirably. Where she used to give us Corots and Daubignys, she gives us now exquisite Monets and entrancing Pisaros. Indeed, there are moments, rare, it is true, but still to be observed from time to time, when Nature becomes absolutely modern. Of course she is not always to be relied upon. The fact is that she is in this unfortunate position. Art creates an incomparable and unique effect, and, having done so, passes on to other things. Nature, upon the other hand, forgetting that imitation can be made the sincerest form of insult, keeps on repeating this effect until we all become absolutely wearied of it. Nobody of any real culture, for instance, ever talks nowadays about the beauty of a sunset. Sunsets are quite old fashioned. They belong to the time when Turner was the last note in art. To admire them is a distinct sign of provincialism of temperament. Upon the other hand they go on. Yesterday evening Mrs Arundel insisted on my coming to the window, and looking at the glorious sky, as she called it. Of course I had to look at it. She is one of those absurdly pretty Philistines, to whom one can deny nothing. And what was it? It was simply a very second-rate Turner, a Turner of a bad period, with all the painter's worst faults exaggerated and over-emphasized. Of course, I am quite ready to admit that Life very often commits the same error. She produces her false Renés and her sham Vautrins, just as Nature gives us, on one day a doubtful Cuyp, and on another a more than questionable Rousseau. Still, Nature irritates one more when she does things of that kind. It seems so stupid, so obvious, so unnecessary. A false Vautrin might be delightful. A doubtful Cuyp is unbearable. However, I don't want to be too hard on Nature. I wish the Channel, especially at Hastings, did not look quite so often like a Henry Moore, grey pearl with yellow lights, but then, when Art is more varied, Nature will, no doubt, be more varied also. That she imitates Art, I don't think even her worst enemy would deny now. It is the one thing that keeps her in touch with civilized man. But have I proved my theory to your satisfaction?

CYRIL: You have proved it to my dissatisfaction, which is better. But even admitting this strange imitative instinct in Life and Nature, surely you would acknowledge that Art expresses the temper of its age, the spirit of its time, the moral and social conditions that surround it, and under whose influence it is produced.

VIVIAN: Certainly not! Art never expresses anything but itself . . . The fact is that we look back on the ages entirely through the medium of Art, and Art, very fortunately, has never once told us the truth.

CYRIL: But modern portraits by English painters, what of them? Surely they are like the people they pretend to represent?

VIVIAN: Quite so. They are so like them that a hundred years from now no one will believe in them. The only portraits in which one believes are portraits where there is very little of the sitter and a very great deal of the artist. Holbein's drawings of the men and women of his time impress us with a sense of their absolute reality. But this is simply because Holbein compelled life to accept his conditions, to restrain itself within his limitations, to reproduce his type, and to appear as he wished it to appear. It is style that makes us believe in a thing – nothing but style. Most of our modern portrait painters are doomed to absolute oblivion. They never paint what they see. They paint what the public sees, and the public never sees anything.

CYRIL: Well, after that I think I should like to hear the end of your article.

VIVIAN: With pleasure. Whether it will do any good I really cannot say. Ours is certainly the dullest and most prosaic century possible. Why, even Sleep has played us false, and has closed up the gates of ivory, and opened the gates of horn. The dreams of the great middle classes of this country, as recorded in Mr Myers's two bulky volumes on the subject and in the *Transactions of the Psychical Society*, are the most depressing things that I have ever read. There is not even a fine nightmare among them. They are commonplace, sordid, and tedious. As for the Church I cannot conceive anything better for the culture of a country than the presence in it of a body of men whose duty it is to believe in the supernatural, to perform daily miracles, and to keep alive that mythopoetic faculty which is so essential for the imagination. But in the English Church a man succeeds, not through his capacity for belief but through his capacity for disbelief. Ours is the only Church where the sceptic stands at the altar, and where St Thomas is regarded as the ideal apostle. Many a worthy clergyman, who passes his life in admirable works of kindly charity, lives and dies unnoticed and unknown; but it is sufficient for some shallow uneducated passman out of either University to get up in his pulpit and express his doubts about Noah's ark, or Balaam's ass, or Jonah and the whale, for half of London to flock to hear him, and to sit openmouthed in rapt admiration at his superb intellect. The growth of common sense in the English Church is a thing very much to be regretted. It is really a degrading concession to a low form of realism. It is silly, too. It springs from an entire ignorance of psychology. Man can believe the impossible, but man can never believe the improbable. However, I must read the end of my article:

'What we have to do, what at any rate it is our duty to do, is to revive this old art of Lying. Much of course may be done, in the way of educating the public, by amateurs in the domestic circle, at literary lunches, and at afternoon teas. But this is merely the light and graceful side of Lying, such as was probably heard at Cretan dinner-parties. There are many other forms. Lying for the sake of gaining some immediate personal advantage, for instance – lying with a moral purpose, as it is usually called – though of late it has been rather looked down upon, was extremely popular with the antique world. Athena laughs when Odysseus tells her "his words of sly devising", as Mr William Morris phrases it, and the glory of mendacity illumines the pale brow of the stainless hero of Euripidean tragedy, and sets among the noble women of the past the young bride of one of Horace's most exquisite odes. Later on, what at first had been merely a natural instinct was elevated into a self-conscious science. Elaborate rules were laid down for the guidance of mankind, and an important school of literature grew up round the subject. Indeed, when one remembers the excellent philosophical treatise of Sanchez on the whole question one cannot help regretting that no one has ever thought of publishing a cheap and condensed edition of the works of that great casuist. A short primer, "When to Lie and How", if brought out in an attractive and not too expensive a form, would no doubt command a large sale, and would prove of real practical service to many earnest and deep-thinking people. Lying for the sake of the improvement of the young, which is the basis of home education, still lingers amongst us, and its advantages are so admirably set forth in the early books of Plato's *Republic* that it is unnecessary to dwell upon them here. It is a mode of Lying for which all good mothers have peculiar capabilities, but it is capable of still further development, and has been sadly overlooked by the School Board. Lying for the sake of a monthly salary is of course well known in Fleet Street, and the profession of a political leader-writer is not without its advantages. But it is said to be a somewhat dull occupation, and it certainly does not lead to much beyond a kind of ostentatious obscurity. The only form of Lying that is absolutely beyond reproach is Lying for its own sake, and the highest development of this is, as we have already pointed out, Lying in Art. Just as those who do not love Plato more

than Truth cannot pass beyond the threshold of
the Academe, so those who do not love Beauty
more than Truth never know the inmost shrine
of Art. The solid stolid British intellect lies in the
desert sands like the Sphinx in Flaubert's marvellous tale, and fantasy *La Chimère*, dances
round it, and calls to it with her false, flute-toned
voice. It may not hear her now, but surely some
day, when we are all bored to death with the
commonplace character of modern fiction, it
will hearken to her and try to borrow her wings.

'And when that day dawns, or sunset reddens
how joyous we shall all be! Facts will be regarded as
discreditable, Truth will be found mourning over
her fetters, and Romance, with her temper of
wonder, will return to the land. The very aspect of
the world will change to our startled eyes. Out of
the sea will rise Behemoth and Leviathan, and sail
round the high-pooped galleys, as they do on the
delightful maps of those ages when books on
geography were actually readable. Dragons will
wander about the waste places, and the phoenix
will soar from her nest of fire into the air. We shall
lay our hands upon the basilisk, and see the jewel
in the toad's head. Champing his gilded oats, the
Hippogriff will stand in our stalls, and over our
heads will float the Blue Bird singing of beautiful
and impossible things, of things that are lovely

and that never happened, of things that are not and that should be. But before this comes to pass we must cultivate the lost art of Lying.' . . .

The final revelation is that Lying, the telling of beautiful untrue things, is the proper aim of Art. But of this I think I have spoken at sufficient length. And now let us go out on the terrace, where 'droops the milk-white peacock like a ghost', while the evening star 'washes the dusk with silver'. At twilight nature becomes a wonderfully suggestive effect, and is not without loveliness, though perhaps its chief use is to illustrate quotations from the poets. Come! We have talked long enough.

3

The Picture of Dorian Gray

AFTER ABOUT A quarter of an hour Hallward stopped painting, looked for a long time at Dorian Gray, and then for a long time at the picture, biting the end of one of his huge brushes, and frowning. 'It is quite finished,' he cried at last, and stooping down he wrote his name in long vermilion letters on the left-hand corner of the canvas.

Lord Henry came over and examined the picture. It was certainly a wonderful work of art, and a wonderful likeness as well.

'My dear fellow, I congratulate you most warmly,' he said. 'It is the finest portrait of modern times. Mr Gray, come over and look at yourself.'

The lad started, as if awakened from some dream. 'Is it really finished?' he murmured, stepping down from the platform.

'Quite finished,' said the painter. 'And you have sat splendidly today. I am awfully obliged to you.'

'That is entirely due to me,' broke in Lord Henry. 'Isn't it, Mr Gray?'

Dorian made no answer, but passed listlessly in front of his picture, and turned towards it. When he saw it he drew back, and his cheeks flushed for a moment with pleasure. A look of joy came into his eyes, as if he had recognized himself for the first time. He stood there motionless and in wonder, dimly conscious that Hallward was speaking to him, but not catching the meaning of his words. The sense of his own beauty came on him like a revelation. He had never felt it before. Basil Hallward's compliments had seemed to him to be merely the charming exaggerations of friendship. He had listened to them, laughed at them, forgotten them. They had not influenced his nature. Then had come Lord Henry Wotton with his strange panegyric on youth, his terrible warning of its brevity. That had stirred him at the time, and now, as he stood gazing at the shadow of his own loveliness, the full reality of the description flashed across him. Yes, there would be a day when his face would be wrinkled and wizen, his eyes dim and colourless, the grace of his figure broken and deformed. The scarlet would pass away from his lips, and the gold steal from his hair. The life that was to make his soul would mar his body. He would become dreadful, hideous, and uncouth.

As he thought of it, a sharp pang of pain struck through him like a knife, and made each delicate fibre of his nature quiver. His eyes deepened into amethyst, and across them came a mist of tears. He felt as if a hand of ice had been laid upon his heart.

'Don't you like it?' cried Hallward at last, stung a little by the lad's silence, not understanding what it meant.

'Of course he likes it,' said Lord Henry. 'Who wouldn't like it? It is one of the greatest things in modern art. I will give you anything you like to ask for it. I must have it.'

'It is not my property, Harry.'

'Whose property is it?'

'Dorian's, of course,' answered the painter.

'He is a very lucky fellow.'

'How sad it is!' murmured Dorian Gray, with his eyes still fixed upon his own portrait. 'How sad it is! I shall grow old, and horrible, and dreadful. But this picture will remain always young. It will never be older than this particular day of June . . . If it were only the other way! If it were I who was to be always young, and the picture that was to grow old! For that – for that – I would give everything! Yes, there is nothing in the whole world I would not give! I would give my soul for that!'

'You would hardly care for such an arrangement, Basil,' cried Lord Henry, laughing. 'It would be rather hard lines on your work.'

'I should object very strongly, Harry,' said Hallward.

Dorian Gray turned and looked at him. 'I believe you would, Basil. You like your art better than your friends. I am no more to you than a green bronze figure. Hardly as much, I dare say.'

The painter stared in amazement. It was so unlike Dorian to speak like that. What had happened? He seemed quite angry. His face was flushed and his cheeks burning.

'Yes,' he continued, 'I am less to you than your ivory Hermes or your silver Faun. You will like them always. How long will you like me? Till I have my first wrinkle, I suppose. I know, now, that when one loses one's good looks, whatever they may be, one loses everything. Your picture has taught me that. Lord Henry Wotton is perfectly right. Youth is the only thing worth having. When I find that I am growing old, I shall kill myself.'

Hallward turned pale, and caught his hand. 'Dorian! Dorian!' he cried, 'don't talk like that. I have never had such a friend as you, and I shall never have such another. You are not jealous of material things, are you? – you who are finer than any of them!'

'I am jealous of everything whose beauty does not

die. I am jealous of the portrait you have painted of me. Why should it keep what I must lose? Every moment that passes takes something from me, and gives something to it. Oh, if it were only the other way! If the picture would change, and I could be always what I am now! Why did you paint it? It will mock me some day – mock me horribly!' The hot tears welled into his eyes; he tore his hand away, and, flinging himself on the divan, he buried his face in the cushions, as though he was praying.

'This is your doing, Harry,' said the painter, bitterly.

Lord Henry shrugged his shoulders. 'It is the real Dorian Gray – that is all.'

'It is not.'

'If it is not, what have I to do with it?'

'You should have gone away when I asked you,' he muttered.

'I stayed when you asked me,' was Lord Henry's answer.

'Harry, I can't quarrel with my two best friends at once, but between you both you have made me hate the finest piece of work I have ever done, and I will destroy it. What is it but canvas and colour? I will not let it come across our three lives and mar them.'

Dorian Gray lifted his golden head from the pillow, and with pallid face and tear-stained eyes looked at him, as he walked over to the deal painting-table that was set beneath the high curtained window. What was he doing there? His fingers were straying about among the litter of tin tubes and dry brushes, seeking for something. Yes, it was for the long palette-knife, with its thin blade of lithe steel. He had found it at last. He was going to rip up the canvas.

With a stifled sob the lad leaped from the couch, and, rushing over to Hallward, tore the knife out of his hand, and flung it to the end of the studio. 'Don't, Basil, don't!' he cried. 'It would be murder!'

'I am glad you appreciate my work at last, Dorian,' said the painter, coldly, when he had recovered from his surprise. 'I never thought you would.'

'Appreciate it? I am in love with it, Basil. It is part of myself. I feel that.'

'Well, as soon as you are dry, you shall be varnished, and framed, and sent home. Then you can do what you like with yourself.' And he walked across the room and rang the bell for tea. 'You will have tea, of course, Dorian? And so will you, Harry? Or do you object to such simple pleasures?'

*   *   *

'I suppose you have heard the news, Basil?' said Lord Henry that evening, as Hallward was shown into a little private room at the Bristol where dinner had been laid for three.

'No, Harry,' answered the artist, giving his hat and coat to the bowing waiter. 'What is it? Nothing about politics, I hope? They don't interest me. There is hardly a single person in the House of Commons worth painting; though many of them would be the better for a little whitewashing.'

'Dorian Gray is engaged to be married,' said Lord Henry, watching him as he spoke.

Hallward started, and then frowned. 'Dorian engaged to be married!' he cried. 'Impossible!'

'It is perfectly true.'

'To whom?'

'To some little actress or other.'

'I can't believe it. Dorian is far too sensible.'

'Dorian is far too wise not to do foolish things now and then, my dear Basil.'

'Marriage is hardly a thing that one can do now and then, Harry.'

'Except in America,' rejoined Lord Henry, languidly. 'But I didn't say he was married. I said he was engaged to be married. There is a great difference. I have a distinct remembrance of being married, but I have no recollection at all of being engaged. I am inclined to think that I never was engaged.'

'But think of Dorian's birth, and position, and wealth. It would be absurd for him to marry so much beneath him.'

'If you want to make him marry this girl tell him that, Basil. He is sure to do it, then. Whenever a man does a thoroughly stupid thing, it is always from the noblest motives.'

'I hope the girl is good, Harry. I don't want to see Dorian tied up to some vile creature, who might degrade his nature and ruin his intellect.'

'Oh, she is better than good – she is beautiful,' murmured Lord Henry, sipping a glass of vermouth and orange-bitters. 'Dorian says she is beautiful; and he is not often wrong about things of that kind. Your portrait of him has quickened his appreciation of the personal appearance of other people. It has had that excellent effect, amongst others. We are to see her to-night, if that boy doesn't forget his appointment.'

'Are you serious?'

'Quite serious, Basil. I should be miserable if I thought I should ever be more serious than I am at the present moment.'

'But do you approve of it, Harry?' asked the painter, walking up and down the room, and biting his lip. 'You can't approve of it, possibly. It is some silly infatuation.'

'I never approve, or disapprove, of anything now. It is an absurd attitude to take towards life. We are not sent into the world to air our moral prejudices. I never take any notice of what common people say, and I never interfere with what charming people do. If a personality fascinates me, whatever mode of expression that personality selects is absolutely delightful to me. Dorian Gray falls in love with a beautiful girl who acts Juliet, and proposes to marry her. Why not? If he wedded Messalina he would be none the less interesting. You know I am not a champion of marriage. The real drawback to marriage is that it makes one unselfish. And unselfish people are colourless. They lack individuality. Still, there are certain temperaments that marriage makes more complex. They regain their egotism, and add to it many other egos. They are forced to have more than one life. They become more highly organized, and to be highly organized is, I should fancy, the object of man's existence. Besides, every experience is of value, and, whatever one may say against marriage, it is certainly an experience. I hope that Dorian Gray will make this girl his wife, passionately adore her for six months, and then suddenly become fascinated by someone else. He would be a wonderful study.'

'You don't mean a single word of all that, Harry; you know you don't. If Dorian Gray's life were spoiled, no one would be sorrier than yourself. You are much better than you pretend to be.'

Lord Henry laughed. 'The reason we all like to think so well of others is that we are all afraid for ourselves. The basis of optimism is sheer terror. We think that we are generous because we credit our neighbour with the possession of those virtues that are likely to be a benefit to us. We praise the banker that we may overdraw our account, and find good qualities in the highwayman in the hope that he may spare our pockets. I mean everything that I have said. I have the greatest contempt for optimism. As for a spoiled life, no life is spoiled but one whose growth is arrested. If you want to mar a nature, you have merely to reform it. As for marriage, of course that would be silly, but there are other and more interesting bonds between men and women. I will certainly encourage them. They have the charm of being fashionable. But here is Dorian himself. He will tell you more than I can.'

'My dear Harry, my dear Basil, you must both con-gratulate me!' said the lad, throwing off his evening cape with its satin-lined wings and shaking each of his friends by the hand in turn. 'I have never been so happy. Of course it is sudden; all really delightful things are. And yet it seems to me to be the one thing I have been looking for all my life.' He was flushed with excitement and pleasure, and looked extraor-dinarily handsome.

'I hope you will always be very happy, Dorian,' said Hallward, 'but I don't quite forgive you for not having let me know of your engagement. You let Harry know.'

'And I don't forgive you for being late for dinner,' broke in Lord Henry, putting his hand on the lad's shoulder, and smiling as he spoke. 'Come, let us sit down and try what the new *chef* here is like, and then you will tell us how it all came about.'

'There is really not much to tell,' cried Dorian, as they took their seats at the small round table. 'What happened was simply this. After I left you yesterday evening, Harry, I dressed, had some dinner at that little Italian restaurant in Rupert Street you introduced me to, and went down at eight o'clock to the theatre. Sibyl was playing Rosalind. Of course the scenery was dreadful, and the Orlando absurd. But Sibyl! You should have seen her! When she came on in her boy's clothes she was perfectly wonderful. She wore a moss-coloured velvet jerkin with cinnamon sleeves, slim brown cross-gartered hose, a dainty little green cap with a hawk's feather caught in a jewel, and a hooded cloak lined with dull red. She had never seemed to me more exquisite. She had all the delicate grace of that Tanagra figurine that you have in your studio, Basil. Her hair clustered round her face like dark leaves round a pale rose. As for her acting – well, you shall see her tonight. She is simply a born artist. I sat in the dingy box absolutely enthralled. I forgot that I was in London and in the nineteenth century. I was away with my love in a forest that no man had ever seen. After the performance was over I went behind, and spoke to her. As we were sitting together, suddenly there came into her eyes a look that I had never seen there before. My lips moved towards hers. We kissed each other. I can't describe to you what I felt at that moment. It seemed to me that all my life had been narrowed to one perfect point of rose-coloured joy. She trembled all over, and shook like a white narcissus. Then she flung herself on her knees and kissed my hands. I feel that I should not tell you all this, but I can't help it. Of course our engagement is a dead secret. She has not even told her own mother. I don't know what my guardians will say. Lord Radley is sure to be furious. I don't care. I shall be of age in less than a year, and then I can do what I like. I have been right, Basil, haven't I, to take my love out of poetry, and to find my wife in Shakespeare's plays? Lips that Shakespeare taught to speak have whispered their secret in my ear. I have had the arms of Rosalind around me, and kissed Juliet on the mouth.'

'Yes, Dorian, I suppose you were right,' said Hall-ward, slowly.

'Have you seen her today?' asked Lord Henry.

Dorian Gray shook his head. 'I left her in the forest of Arden, I shall find her in an orchard in Verona.'

Lord Henry sipped his champagne in a meditative manner. 'At what particular point did you mention the word marriage, Dorian? And what did she say in answer? Perhaps you forgot all about it.'

'My dear Harry, I did not treat it as a business transaction, and I did not make any formal proposal. I told her that I loved her, and she said she was not worthy to be my wife. Not worthy! Why, the whole world is nothing to me compared with her.'

'Women are wonderfully practical,' murmured Lord Henry – 'much more practical than we are. In situations of that kind we often forget to say anything about marriage, and they always remind us.'

Hallward laid his hand upon his arm. 'Don't, Harry. You have annoyed Dorian. He is not like other men. He would never bring misery upon any one. His nature is too fine for that.'

Lord Henry looked across the table. 'Dorian is never annoyed with me,' he answered. 'I asked the question for the best reason possible, for the only reason, indeed, that excuses one for asking any question – simple curiosity. I have a theory that it is always the women who propose to us, and not we who propose to the women. Except, of course, in middle-class life. But then the middle classes are not modern.'

Dorian Gray laughed, and tossed his head. 'You are quite incorrigible, Harry; but I don't mind. It is impossible to be angry with you. When you see Sibyl Vane you will feel that the man who could wrong her would be a beast, a beast without a heart. I cannot understand how anyone can wish to shame the thing he loves. I love Sibyl Vane. I want to place her on a pedestal of gold, and to see the world worship the woman who is mine. What is marriage? An irrevocable vow. You mock at it for that. Ah! don't mock. It is an irrevocable vow that I want to take. Her trust makes me faithful, her belief makes me good. When I am with her, I regret all that you have taught me. I become different from what you have known me to be. I am changed, and the mere touch of Sibyl Vane's hand makes me forget you and all your wrong, fascinating, poisonous, delightful theories.'

'And those are . . .?' asked Lord Henry, helping himself to some salad.

'Oh, your theories about life, your theories about love, your theories about pleasure. All your theories, in fact, Harry.'

'Pleasure is the only thing worth having a theory about,' he answered, in his slow, melodious voice. 'But I am afraid I cannot claim my theory as my own. It belongs to Nature, not to me. Pleasure is Nature's test, her sign of approval. When we are happy we are always good, but when we are good we are not always happy.'

'Ah! but what do you mean by good?' cried Basil Hallward.

'Yes,' echoed Dorian, leaning back in his chair, and looking at Lord Henry over the heavy clusters of purple-lipped irises that stood in the centre of the table, 'what do you mean by good, Harry?'

'To be good is to be in harmony with oneself,' he replied, touching the thin stem of his glass with his pale, fine-pointed fingers. 'Discord is to be forced to be in harmony with others. One's own life – that is the important thing. As for the lives of one's neighbours, if one wishes to be a prig or a Puritan, one can flaunt one's moral views about them, but they are not one's concern. Besides, Individualism has really the higher aim. Modern morality consists in accepting the standard of one's age. I consider that for any man of culture to accept the standard of his age is a form of the grossest immorality.'

'But, surely, if one lives merely for oneself, Harry, one pays a terrible price for doing so?' suggested the painter.

'Yes, we are overcharged for everything nowadays. I should fancy that the real tragedy of the poor is that they can afford nothing but self-denial. Beautiful sins, like beautiful things, are the privilege of the rich.'

'One has to pay in other ways but money.'

'What sort of ways, Basil?'

'Oh! I should fancy in remorse, in suffering, in . . . well, in the consciousness of degradation.'

Lord Henry shrugged his shoulders. 'My dear fellow, medieval art is charming, but medieval emotions are out of date. One can use them in fiction, of course. But then the only things that one can use in fiction are the things that one has ceased to use in fact. Believe me, no civilized man ever regrets a pleasure, and no uncivilized man ever knows what a pleasure is.'

'I know what pleasure is,' cried Dorian Gray. 'It is to adore someone.'

'That is certainly better than being adored,' he answered, toying with some fruits. 'Being adored is a nuisance. Women treat us just as Humanity treats its gods. They worship us, and are always bothering us to do something for them.'

'I should have said that whatever they ask for they had first given to us,' murmured the lad, gravely. 'They create Love in our natures. They have a right to demand it back.'

'That is quite true, Dorian,' cried Hallward.

'Nothing is ever quite true,' said Lord Henry.

'This is,' interrupted Dorian. 'You must admit, Harry, that women give to men the very gold of their lives.'

'Possibly,' he sighed, 'but they invariably want it back in such very small change. That is the worry. Women, as some witty Frenchman once put it, inspire us with the desire to do masterpieces, and always prevent us from carrying them out.'

'Harry, you are dreadful! I don't know why I like you so much.'

'You will always like me, Dorian,' he replied. 'Will you have some coffee, you fellows? – Waiter, bring coffee, and *fine-champagne,* and some cigarettes. No: don't mind the cigarettes; I have some. Basil, I can't allow you to smoke cigars. You must have a cigarette. A cigarette is the perfect type of a perfect pleasure. It is exquisite, and it leaves one unsatisfied. What more can one want? Yes, Dorian, you will always be fond of me. I represent to you all the sins you have never had the courage to commit.'

'What nonsense you talk, Harry!' cried the lad, taking a light from a fire-breathing silver dragon that the waiter had placed on the table. 'Let us go down to the theatre. When Sibyl comes on the stage you will have a new ideal of life. She will represent something to you that you have never known.'

'I have known everything,' said Lord Henry, with a tired look in his eyes, 'but I am always ready for a new emotion. I am afraid, however, that, for me at any rate, there is no such thing. Still, your wonderful girl may thrill me. I love acting. It is so much more real than life. Let us go. Dorian, you will come with me. I am so sorry, Basil, but there is only room for two in the brougham. You must follow us in a hansom.'

They got up and put on their coats, sipping their coffee standing. The painter was silent and preoccupied. There was a gloom over him. He could not bear this marriage, and yet it seemed to him to be better than many other things that might have happened.

After a few minutes, they all passed downstairs. He drove off by himself, as had been arranged, and watched the flashing lights of the little brougham in front of him. A strange sense of loss came over him. He felt that Dorian Gray would never again be to him all that he had been in the past. Life had come between them ... His eyes darkened, and the crowded, flaring streets became blurred to his eyes. When the cab drew up at the theatre, it seemed to him that he had grown years older.

* * *

FOR SOME REASON or other, the house was crowded that night, and the fat Jew manager who met them at the door was beaming from ear to ear with an oily, tremulous smile. He escorted them to their box with a sort of pompous humility, waving his fat jew-elled hands, and talking at the top of his voice. Dorian Gray loathed him more than ever. He felt as if he had come to look for Miranda and had been met by Caliban. Lord Henry, upon the other hand, rather liked him. At least he declared he did, and insisted on shaking him by the hand, and assuring him that he was proud to meet a man who had discovered a real genius and gone bankrupt over a poet. Hallward amused himself with watching the faces in the pit. The heat was terribly oppressive, and the huge sun-light flamed like a monstrous dahlia with petals of yellow fire. The youths in the gallery had taken off their coats and waistcoats and hung them over the side. They talked to each other across the theatre, and shared their oranges with the tawdry girls who sat beside them. Some women were laughing in the pit. Their voices were horribly shrill and discordant. The sound of the popping of corks came from the bar.

'What a place to find one's divinity in!' said Lord Henry.

'Yes!' answered Dorian Gray. 'It was here I found her, and she is divine beyond all living things. When she acts you will forget everything. These common, rough people, with their coarse faces and brutal gestures, become quite different when she is on the stage. They sit silently and watch her. They weep and laugh as she wills them to do. She makes them as responsive as a violin. She spiritualizes them, and one feels that they are of the same flesh and blood as oneself.'

'The same flesh and blood as oneself! Oh, I hope not!' exclaimed Lord Henry, who was scanning the occupants of the gallery through his opera-glass.

'Don't pay any attention to him, Dorian,' said the painter. 'I understand what you mean, and I believe in this girl. Anyone you love must be marvellous, and any girl that has the effect you describe must be fine and noble. To spiritualize one's age – that is something worth doing. If this girl can give a soul to those who have lived without one, if she can create the sense of beauty in people whose lives have been sordid and ugly, if she can strip them of their selfishness and lend them tears for sorrows that are not their own, she is worthy of all your adoration, worthy of the adoration of the world. This marriage is quite right. I did not think so at first, but I admit it now. The gods made Sibyl Vane for you. Without her you would have been incomplete.'

'Thanks, Basil,' answered Dorian Gray, pressing his hand. 'I knew that you would understand me. Harry is so cynical, he terrifies me. But here is the orchestra. It is quite dreadful, but it only lasts for about five minutes. Then the curtain rises, and you will see the girl to whom I am going to give all my life, to whom I have given everything that is good in me.'

A quarter of an hour afterwards, amidst an extra-ordinary turmoil of applause, Sibyl Vane stepped on to the stage. Yes, she was certainly lovely to look at – one of the loveliest creatures, Lord Henry thought, that he had ever seen. There was something of the fawn in her shy glance and startled eyes. A faint blush, like the shadow of a rose in a mirror of silver, came to her cheeks as she glanced at the crowded, enthusiastic house. She stepped back a few paces, and her lips seemed to tremble. Basil Hallward leaped to his feet and began to applaud. Motionless, and as one in a dream, sat Dorian Gray, gazing at her. Lord

Henry peered through his glasses, murmuring, 'Charming! charming!'

The scene was the hall of Capulet's house, and Romeo in his pilgrim's dress had entered with Mercutio and his other friends. The band, such as it was, struck up a few bars of music, and the dance began. Through the crowd of ungainly, shabbily dressed actors, Sibyl Vane moved like a creature from a finer world. Her body swayed, while she danced, as a plant sways in the water. The curves of her throat were the curves of a white lily. Her hands seemed to be made of cool ivory.

Yet she was curiously listless. She showed no sign of joy when her eyes rested on Romeo. The few words she had to speak:

> Good pilgrim, you do wrong your hand too much,
> Which mannerly devotion shows in this;
> For saints have hands that pilgrims' hands do touch,
> And palm to palm is holy palmers' kiss—

with the brief dialogue that follows, were spoken in a thoroughly artificial manner. The voice was exquisite, but from the point of view of tone it was absolutely false. It was wrong in colour. It took away all the life from the verse. It made the passion unreal.

Dorian Gray grew pale as he watched her. He was puzzled and anxious. Neither of his friends dared to say anything to him. She seemed to them to be absolutely incompetent. They were horribly disappointed.

Yet they felt that the true test of any Juliet is the balcony scene of the second act. They waited for that. If she failed there, there was nothing in her.

She looked charming as she came out in the moonlight. That could not be denied. But the staginess of her acting was unbearable, and grew worse as she went on. Her gestures became absurdly artificial. She over-emphasized everything that she had to say. The beautiful passage:

> Thou knowest the mask of night is on my face,
> Else would a maiden blush bepaint my cheek
> For that which thou hast heard me speak tonight—

was declaimed with the painful precision of a schoolgirl who has been taught to recite by some second-rate professor of elocution. When she leaned over the balcony and came to those wonderful lines:

> Although I joy in thee,
> I have no joy of this contract tonight:
> It is too rash, too unadvised, too sudden;
> Too like the lightning, which doth cease to be
> Ere one can say, 'It lightens.' Sweet, goodnight!
> This bud of love by summer's ripening breath
> May prove a beauteous flower when next we meet—

she spoke the words as though they conveyed no meaning to her. It was not nervousness. Indeed, so far from being nervous, she was absolutely self-contained. It was simply bad art. She was a complete failure.

Even the common, uneducated audience of the pit and gallery lost their interest in the play. They got restless, and began to talk loudly and to whistle. The Jew manager, who was standing at the back of the dress-circle, stamped and swore with rage. The only person unmoved was the girl herself.

When the second act was over there came a storm of hisses, and Lord Henry got up from his chair and put on his coat. 'She is quite beautiful, Dorian,' he said, 'but she can't act. Let us go.'

'I am going to see the play through,' answered the lad, in a hard, bitter voice. 'I am awfully sorry that I have made you waste an evening, Harry. I apologize to you both.'

'My dear Dorian, I should think Miss Vane was ill,' interrupted Hallward. 'We will come some other night.'

'I wish she were ill,' he rejoined. 'But she seems to me to be simply callous and cold. She has entirely altered. Last night she was a great artist. This evening she is merely a commonplace, mediocre actress.'

'Don't talk like that about anyone you love, Dorian. Love is a more wonderful thing than Art.'

'They are both simply forms of imitation,' remarked Lord Henry. 'But do let us go. Dorian, you must not stay here any longer. It is not good for one's morals to see bad acting. Besides, I don't suppose you will want your wife to act. So what does it matter if she plays Juliet like a wooden doll? She is very lovely, and if she knows as little about life as she does about acting, she will be a delightful experience. There are only two kinds of people who are really fascinating – people who know absolutely everything, and people who know absolutely nothing. Good heavens, my dear boy, don't look so tragic! The secret of remaining young is never to have an emotion that is unbecoming. Come to the club with Basil and myself. We will smoke cigarettes and drink to the beauty of Sibyl Vane. She is beautiful. What more can you want?'

'Go away, Harry,' cried the lad. 'I want to be alone. Basil, you must go. Ah! can't you see that my heart is breaking?' The hot tears came to his eyes. His lips trembled, and, rushing to the back of the box, he leaned up against the wall, hiding his face in his hands.

'Let us go, Basil,' said Lord Henry, with a strange tenderness in his voice; and the two young men passed out together.

A few moments afterwards the footlights flared up, and the curtain rose on the third act. Dorian Gray went back to his seat. He looked pale, and proud, and indifferent. The play dragged on, and seemed interminable. Half of the audience went out, tramping in heavy boots, and laughing. The whole thing was a fiasco. The last act was played to almost empty benches. The curtain went down on a titter, and some groans.

As soon as it was over, Dorian Gray rushed behind the scenes into the green-room. The girl was standing there alone, with a look of triumph on her face. Her eyes were lit with an exquisite fire. There was a radiance about her. Her parted lips were smiling over some secret of their own.

When he entered, she looked at him, and an expression of infinite joy came over her. 'How badly I acted tonight, Dorian!' she cried.

'Horribly!' he answered, gazing at her in amazement – 'horribly! It was dreadful. Are you ill? You have no idea what it was. You have no idea what I suffered.'

The girl smiled. 'Dorian,' she answered, lingering over his name with long-drawn music in her voice, as though it were sweeter than honey to the red petals of her mouth – 'Dorian, you should have understood. But you understand now, don't you?'

'Understand what?' he asked, angrily.

'Why I was so bad tonight. Why I shall always be bad. Why I shall never act well again.'

He shrugged his shoulders. 'You are ill, I suppose.

When you are ill you shouldn't act. You make your-self ridiculous. My friends were bored. I was bored.'

She seemed not to listen to him. She was transfig-ured with joy. An ecstasy of happiness dominated her.

'Dorian, Dorian,' she cried, 'before I knew you, acting was the one reality of my life. It was only in the theatre that I lived. I thought that it was all true. I was Rosalind one night, and Portia the other. The joy of Beatrice was my joy, and the sorrows of Cord-elia were mine also. I believed in everything. The common people who acted with me seemed to me to be god-like. The painted scenes were my world. I knew nothing but shadows, and I thought them real. You came – oh, my beautiful love! – and you freed my soul from prison. You taught me what reality really is. Tonight, for the first time in my life, I saw through the hollowness, the sham, the silliness of the empty pageant in which I had always played. Tonight, for the first time, I became conscious that the Romeo was hideous, and old, and painted, that the moon-light in the orchard was false, that the scenery was vulgar, and that the words I had to speak were unreal, were not my words, were not what I wanted to say. You had brought me something higher, something of which all art is but a reflection. You had made me understand what love really is. My love! my love! Prince Charming! Prince of Life! I have grown sick of shadows. You are more to me than all art can ever be. What have I to do with the puppets of a play? When I came on tonight, I could not understand how it was that everything had gone from me. I thought that I was going to be wonderful. I found that I could do nothing. Suddenly it dawned on my soul what it all meant. The knowledge was exquisite to me. I heard them hissing, and I smiled. What could they know of love such as ours? Take me away, Dorian – take me away with you, where we can be quite alone. I hate the stage. I might mimic a passion that I do not feel, but I cannot mimic one that burns me like fire. Oh, Dorian, Dorian, you understand now what it signifies? Even if I could do it, it would be profanation for me to play at being in love. You have made me see that.'

He flung himself down on the sofa, and turned away his face. 'You have killed my love,' he muttered.

She looked at him in wonder, and laughed. He made no answer. She came across to him, and with her little fingers stroked his hair. She knelt down and pressed his hands to her lips. He drew them away, and a shudder ran through him.

Then he leaped up, and went to the door. 'Yes,' he cried, 'you have killed my love. You used to stir my imagination. Now you don't even stir my curiosity. You simply produce no effect. I loved you because you were marvellous, because you had genius and intellect, because you realized the dreams of great poets and gave shape and substance to the shadows of art. You have thrown it all away. You are shallow and stupid. My God! how mad I was to love you! What a fool I have been! You are nothing to me now. I will never see you again. I will never think of you. I will never mention your name. You don't know what you were to me, once. Why, once . . . Oh, I can't bear to think of it! I wish I had never laid eyes upon you! You have spoiled the romance of my life. How little you can know of love, if you say it mars your art! Without your art you are nothing. I would have made you famous, splendid, magnificent. The world would have worshipped you, and you would have borne my name. What are you now? A third-rate actress with a pretty face.'

The girl grew white, and trembled. She clenched her hands together, and her voice seemed to catch in her throat. 'You are not serious, Dorian?' she murmured. 'You are acting.'

'Acting! I leave that to you. You do it so well,' he answered bitterly.

She rose from her knees, and, with a piteous expression of pain in her face, came across the room to him. She put her hand upon his arm, and looked into his eyes. He thrust her back. 'Don't touch me!' he cried.

A low moan broke from her, and she flung herself at his feet, and lay there like a trampled flower.

'Dorian, Dorian, don't leave me!' she whispered. 'I am so sorry I didn't act well. I was thinking of you all the time. But I will try – indeed, I will try. It came so suddenly across me, my love for you. I think I should never have known it if you had not kissed me – if we had not kissed each other. Kiss me again, my love. Don't go away from me. I couldn't bear it. Oh! don't go away from me. My brother . . . No; never mind. He didn't mean it. He was in jest . . . But you, oh! can't you forgive me for tonight? I will work so hard, and try to improve. Don't be cruel to me because I love you better than anything in the world. After all, it is only once that I have not pleased you. But you are quite right, Dorian. I should have shown myself more of an artist. It was foolish of me; and yet I couldn't help it. Oh, don't leave me, don't leave me.' A fit of passionate sobbing choked her. She crouched on the floor like a wounded thing, and Dorian Gray, with his beautiful eyes, looked down at her, and his chiselled lips curled in exquisite disdain. There is always something ridiculous about the emotions of people whom one has ceased to love. Sibyl Vane seemed to him to be absurdly melodramatic. Her tears and sobs annoyed him.

'I am going,' he said at last, in his calm, clear voice. 'I don't wish to be unkind, but I can't see you again. You have disappointed me.'

She wept silently, and made no answer, but crept

nearer. Her little hands stretched blindly out, and appeared to be seeking for him. He turned on his heel, and left the room. In a few moments he was out of the theatre.

Where he went to he hardly knew. He remembered wandering through dimly-lit streets, past gaunt black-shadowed archways and evil-looking houses. Women with hoarse voices and harsh laughter had called after him. Drunkards had reeled by cursing, and chattering to themselves like monstrous apes. He had seen grotesque children huddled upon door-steps, and heard shrieks and oaths from gloomy courts.

As the dawn was just breaking he found himself close to Covent Garden. The darkness lifted, and, flushed with faint fires, the sky hollowed itself into a perfect pearl. Huge carts filled with nodding lilies rumbled slowly down the polished empty street. The air was heavy with the perfume of the flowers, and their beauty seemed to bring him an anodyne for his pain. He followed into the market, and watched the men unloading their wagons. A white-smocked carter offered him some cherries. He thanked him, and wondered why he refused to accept any money for them, and began to eat them listlessly. They had been plucked at midnight, and the coldness of the moon had entered into them. A long line of boys carrying crates of striped tulips, and of yellow and red roses, defiled in front of him, threading their way through the huge jade-green piles of vegetables. Under the portico, with its grey sun-bleached pillars, loitered a troop of draggled bareheaded girls, waiting for the auction to be over. Others crowded round the swinging doors of the coffee-house in the Piazza. The heavy cart-horses slipped and stamped upon the rough stones, shaking their bells and trappings. Some of the drivers were lying asleep on a pile of sacks. Iris-necked, and pink-footed, the pigeons ran about picking up seeds.

After a little while, he hailed a hansom, and drove home. For a few moments he loitered upon the door-step, looking round at the silent Square with its blank, close-shuttered windows, and its staring blinds. The sky was pure opal now, and the roofs of the houses glistened like silver against it. From some chimney opposite a thin wreath of smoke was rising. It curled, a violet riband, through the nacre-coloured air.

In the huge gilt Venetian lantern, spoil of some Doge's barge, that hung from the ceiling of the great oak-panelled hall of entrance, lights were still burning from three flickering jets: thin blue petals of flame they seemed, rimmed with white fire. He turned them out, and, having thrown his hat and cape on the table, passed through the library towards the door of his bedroom, a large octagonal chamber on the ground floor that, in his new-born feeling for luxury, he had just had decorated for himself, and hung with some curious Renaissance tapestries that had been discovered stored in a dis-used attic at Selby Royal. As he was turning the handle of the door, his eye fell upon the portrait Basil Hallward had painted of him. He started back as if in surprise. Then he went on into his own room, looking somewhat puzzled. After he had taken the buttonhole out of his coat, he seemed to hesitate. Finally he came back, went over to the pic-ture, and examined it. In the dim arrested light that struggled through the cream-coloured silk blinds, the face appeared to him to be a little changed. The expression looked different. One would have said that there was a touch of cruelty in the mouth. It was certainly strange.

He turned round, and, walking to the window, drew up the blind. The bright dawn flooded the room, and swept the fantastic shadows into dusky corners, where they lay shuddering. But the strange expression that he had noticed in the face of the por-trait seemed to linger there, to be more intensified even. The quivering, ardent sunlight showed him the lines of cruelty round the mouth as clearly as if he had been looking into a mirror after he had done some dreadful thing.

He winced, and, taking up from the table an oval

glass framed in ivory Cupids, one of Lord Henry's many presents to him, glanced hurriedly into its polished depths. No line like that warped his red lips. What did it mean?

He rubbed his eyes, and came close to the picture, and examined it again. There were no signs of any change when he looked into the actual painting, and yet there was no doubt that the whole expression had altered. It was not a mere fancy of his own. The thing was horribly apparent.

He threw himself into a chair, and began to think. Suddenly there flashed across his mind what he had said in Basil Hallward's studio the day the picture had been finished. Yes, he remembered it perfectly. He had uttered a mad wish that he himself might remain young, and the portrait grow old; that his own beauty might be untarnished, and the face on the canvas bear the burden of his passions and his sins; that the painted image might be seared with the lines of suffering and thought, and that he might keep all the delicate bloom and loveliness of his then just conscious boyhood. Surely his wish had not been fulfilled? Such things were impossible. It seemed monstrous even to think of them. And, yet, there was the picture before him, with the touch of cruelty in the mouth.

Cruelty! Had he been cruel? It was the girl's fault, not his. He had dreamed of her as a great artist, had given his love to her because he had thought her great. Then she had disappointed him. She had been shallow and unworthy. And, yet, a feeling of infinite regret came over him, as he thought of her lying at his feet sobbing like a little child. He remembered with what callousness he had watched her. Why had he been made like that? Why had such a soul been given to him? But he had suffered also. During the three terrible hours that the play had lasted, he had lived centuries of pain, æon upon æon of torture. His life was well worth hers. She had marred him for a moment, if he had wounded her for an age. Besides, women were better suited to bear sorrow than men. They lived on their emotions. They only thought of their emotions. When they took lovers, it was merely to have someone with whom they could have scenes. Lord Henry had told him that, and Lord Henry knew what women were. Why should he trouble about Sibyl Vane? She was nothing to him now.

But the picture? What was he to say of that? It held the secret of his life, and told his story. It had taught him to love his own beauty. Would it teach him to loathe his own soul? Would he ever look at it again?

No; it was merely an illusion wrought on the troubled senses. The horrible night that he had passed had left phantoms behind it. Suddenly there had fallen upon his brain that tiny scarlet speck that makes men mad. The picture had not changed. It was folly to think so.

Yet it was watching him, with its beautiful marred face and its cruel smile. Its bright hair gleamed in the early sunlight. Its blue eyes met his own. A sense of infinite pity, not for himself, but for the painted image of himself, came over him. It had altered already, and would alter more. Its gold would wither into grey. Its red and white roses would die. For every sin that he committed, a stain would fleck and wreck its fairness. But he would not sin. The picture, changed or unchanged, would be to him the visible emblem of conscience. He would resist temptation. He would not see Lord Henry anymore – would not, at any rate, listen to those subtle poisonous theories that in Basil Hallward's garden had first stirred within him the passion for impossible things. He would go back to Sibyl Vane, make her amends, marry her, try to love her again. Yes, it was his duty to do so. She must have suffered more than he had. Poor child! He had been selfish and cruel to her. The fascination that she had exercised over him would return. They would be happy together. His life with her would be beautiful and pure.

He got up from his chair, and drew a large screen right in front of the portrait, shuddering as he glanced at it. 'How horrible!' he murmured to himself, and he walked across to the window and opened it. When he stepped out on to the grass, he drew a deep breath. The fresh morning air seemed to drive away all his sombre passions. He thought only of Sibyl. A faint echo of his love came back to him. He repeated her name over and over again. The birds that were singing in the dew-drenched garden seemed to be telling the flowers about her.

*   *   *

'YOU MUST DO me a drawing of Sibyl, Basil. I should like to have something more of her than the memory of a few kisses and some broken pathetic words.'

'I will try and do something, Dorian, if it would please you. But you must come and sit to me yourself again. I can't get on without you.'

'I can never sit to you again, Basil. It is impossible!' he exclaimed, starting back.

The painter stared at him. 'My dear boy, what nonsense!' he cried. 'Do you mean to say you don't like what I did of you? Where is it? Why have you pulled the screen in front of it? Let me look at it. It is the best thing I have ever done. Do take the screen away, Dorian. It is simply disgraceful of your servant hiding my work like that. I felt the room looked different as I came in.'

'My servant has nothing to do with it, Basil. You don't imagine I let him arrange my room for me? He settles my flowers for me sometimes – that is all. No; I did it myself. The light was too strong on the portrait.'

'Too strong! Surely not, my dear fellow? It is an admirable place for it. Let me see it.' And Hallward walked towards the corner of the room.

A cry of terror broke from Dorian Gray's lips, and he rushed between the painter and the screen. 'Basil,' he said, looking very pale, 'you must not look at it. I don't wish you to.'

'Not look at my own work! you are not serious. Why shouldn't I look at it?' exclaimed Hallward, laughing.

'If you try to look at it, Basil, on my word of honour I will never speak to you again as long as I live. I am quite serious. I don't offer any explanation, and you are not to ask for any. But, remember, if you touch this screen, everything is over between us.'

Hallward was thunderstruck. He looked at Dorian Gray in absolute amazement. He had never seen him like this before. The lad was actually pallid with rage. His hands were clenched, and the pupils of his eyes were like disks of blue fire. He was trembling all over.

'Dorian!'

'Don't speak!'

'But what is the matter? Of course I won't look at it if you don't want me to,' he said, rather coldly, turning on his heel, and going over towards the window. 'But, really, it seems rather absurd that I shouldn't see my own work, especially as I am going to exhibit it in Paris in the autumn. I shall probably have to give it another coat of varnish before that, so I must see it some day, and why not today?'

'To exhibit it? You want to exhibit it?' exclaimed Dorian Gray, a strange sense of terror creeping over him. Was the world going to be shown his secret? Were people to gape at the mystery of his life? That was impossible. Something – he did not know what – had to be done at once.

'Yes; I don't suppose you will object to that. Georges Petit is going to collect all my best pictures for a special exhibition in the Rue de Sèze, which will open the first week in October. The portrait will only be away a month. I should think you could easily spare it for that time. In fact, you are sure to be out of town. And if you keep it always behind a screen, you can't care much about it.'

Dorian Gray passed his hand over his forehead. There were beads of perspiration there. He felt that he was on the brink of a horrible danger. 'You told me a month ago that you would never exhibit it,' he cried. 'Why have you changed your mind? You people who go in for being consistent have just as many moods as others have. The only difference is that your moods are rather meaningless. You can't have forgotten that you assured me most solemnly that nothing in the world would induce you to send it to any exhibition. You told Harry exactly the same thing.' He stopped suddenly, and a gleam of light came into his eyes. He remembered that Lord Henry had said to him once, half seriously and half in jest, 'If you want to have a strange quarter of an hour, get Basil to tell you why he won't exhibit your picture. He told me why he wouldn't, and it was a revelation to me.' Yes, perhaps Basil, too, had his secret. He would ask him and try.

'Basil,' he said, coming over quite close, and looking him straight in the face, 'we have each of us a secret. Let me know yours and I shall tell you mine. What was your reason for refusing to exhibit my picture?'

The painter shuddered in spite of himself. 'Dorian, if I told you, you might like me less than you do, and you would certainly laugh at me. I could not bear your doing either of those two things. If you wish me never to look at your picture again, I am content. I have always you to look at. If you wish the best work I have ever done to be hidden from the world, I am satisfied. Your friendship is dearer to me than any fame or reputation.'

'No, Basil, you must tell me,' insisted Dorian Gray. 'I think I have a right to know.' His feeling of terror had passed away, and curiosity had taken its place. He was determined to find out Basil Hallward's mystery.

'Let us sit down, Dorian,' said the painter, looking troubled. 'Let us sit down. And just answer me one question. Have you noticed in the picture something curious? – something that probably at first did not strike you, but that revealed itself to you suddenly?'

'Basil!' cried the lad, clutching the arms of his chair with trembling hands, and gazing at him with wild, startled eyes.

'I see you did. Don't speak. Wait till you hear what I have to say. Dorian, from the moment I met you, your personality had the most extraordinary influence over me. I was dominated, soul, brain and power by you. You became to me the visible incarnation of that unseen ideal whose memory haunts us artists like an exquisite dream. I worshipped you. I grew jealous of everyone to whom you spoke. I wanted to have you all to myself. I was only happy when I was with you. When you were away from me you were still present in my art . . . Of course I never let you know anything about this. It would have been impossible. You would not have understood it. I hardly understood it myself. I only knew that I had seen perfection face to face, and that the world had become wonderful to my eyes – too wonderful, perhaps, for in such mad worships there is peril, the peril of losing them, no less than the peril of keeping them . . . Weeks and weeks went on, and I grew more and more absorbed in you. Then came a new development. I had drawn you as Paris in dainty armour, and as Adonis with huntsman's cloak and polished boar-spear. Crowned with heavy lotus-blossoms you had sat on the prow of Adrian's barge, gazing across the green turbid Nile. You had leant over the still pool of some Greek woodland, and seen in the water's silent silver the marvel of your own face. And it had all been what art should be, unconscious, ideal, and remote. One day, a fatal day I sometimes think, I determined to paint a wonderful portrait of you as you actually are, not in the costume of dead ages, but in your own dress and in your own time. Whether it was the realism of the method, or the mere wonder of your own personality, thus directly presented to me without mist or veil, I cannot tell. But I know that as I worked at it, every flake and film of colour seemed to me to reveal my secret. I grew afraid that others would know of my idolatry. I felt, Dorian, that I had told too much, that I had put too much of myself into it. Then it was that I resolved never to allow the picture to be exhibited. You were a little annoyed; but then you did not realize all that it meant to me. Harry, to whom I talked about it, laughed at me. But I did not mind that. When the picture was finished, and I sat alone with it, I felt that I was right . . . Well, after a few days the thing left my studio, and as soon as I had got rid of the intolerable fascination of its presence, it seemed to me that I had been foolish in imagining that I had seen anything in it, more than that you were extremely good-looking, and that I could paint. Even now I cannot help feeling that it is a mistake to think that the passion one feels in creation is ever really shown in the work one creates. Art is always more abstract than we fancy. Form and colour tell us of form and colour – that is all. It often seems to me that art conceals the artist far more completely than it ever reveals him. And so when I got this offer from Paris I determined to make your portrait the principal thing in my exhibition. It never occurred to me that you would refuse. I see now that you were right. The picture cannot be shown. You must not be angry with me, Dorian, for what I have told you. As I said to Harry, once, you are made to be worshipped.'

Dorian Gray drew a long breath. The colour came back to his cheeks, and a smile played about his lips. The peril was over. He was safe for the time. Yet he could not help feeling infinite pity for the painter who had just made this strange confession to him, and wondered if he himself would ever be so dominated by the personality of a friend. Lord Henry had the charm of being very dangerous. But that was all. He was too clever and too cynical to be really fond of. Would there ever be someone who would fill him with a strange idolatry? Was that one of the things that life had in store?

'It is extraordinary to me, Dorian,' said Hallward, 'that you should have seen this in the portrait. Did you really see it?'

'I saw something in it,' he answered, 'something that seemed to me very curious.'

'Well, you don't mind my looking at the thing now?'

Dorian shook his head. 'You must not ask me that, Basil. I could not possibly let you stand in front of that picture.'

'You will some day, surely?'

'Never.'

'Well, perhaps you are right. And now goodbye, Dorian. You have been the one person in my life who has really influenced my art. Whatever I have done that is good, I owe to you. Ah! you don't know what it cost me to tell you all that I have told you.'

'My dear Basil,' said Dorian, 'what have you told me? Simply that you felt that you admired me too much. That is not even a compliment.'

'It was not intended as a compliment. It was a confession. Now that I have made it, something seems to have gone out of me. Perhaps one should never put one's worship into words.'

'It was a very disappointing confession.'

'Why, what did you expect, Dorian? You didn't see anything else in the picture, did you? There was nothing else to see?'

'No; there was nothing else to see. Why do you ask? But you mustn't talk about worship. It is foolish. You and I are friends, Basil, and we must always remain so.'

'You have got Harry,' said the painter, sadly.

'Oh, Harry!' cried the lad, with a ripple of laughter. 'Harry spends his days in saying what is incredible, and his evenings in doing what is improbable. Just the sort of life I would like to lead. But still I don't think I would go to Harry if I were in trouble. I would sooner go to you, Basil.'

'You will sit to me again?'

'Impossible!'

'You spoil my life as an artist by refusing, Dorian. No man came across two ideal things. Few come across one.'

'I can't explain it to you, Basil, but I must never sit to you again. There is something fatal about a portrait. It has a life of its own. I will come and have tea with you. That will be just as pleasant.'

'Pleasanter for you, I am afraid,' murmured Hallward, regretfully. 'And now goodbye. I am sorry you won't let me look at the picture once again. But that can't be helped. I quite understand what you feel about it.'

As he left the room, Dorian Gray smiled to himself. Poor Basil! how little he knew of the true reason! And how strange it was that, instead of having been forced to reveal his own secret, he had succeeded, almost by chance, in wresting a secret from his friend! How much that strange confession explained to him! The painter's absurd fits of jealousy, his wild devotion, his extravagant panegyrics, his curious reticences – he understood them all now, and he felt sorry. There seemed to him to be something tragic in a friendship so coloured by romance.

He sighed, and touched the bell. The portrait must be hidden away at all costs. He could not run such a risk of discovery again. It had been mad of him to have allowed the thing to remain, even for an hour, in a room to which any of his friends had access.

*   *   *

WHEN HIS SERVANT entered, he looked at him steadfastly, and wondered if he had thought of peering behind the screen. The man was quite impassive, and waited for his orders. Dorian lit a cigarette, and walked over to the glass and glanced into it. He could see the reflection of Victor's face perfectly. It was like a placid mask of servility. There was nothing to be afraid of, there. Yet he thought it best to be on his guard.

Speaking very slowly, he told him to tell the housekeeper that he wanted to see her, and then to go to the frame-maker and ask him to send two of his men round at once. It seemed to him that as the man left the room his eyes wandered in the direction of the screen. Or was that merely his own fancy?

After a few moments, in her black silk dress, with

old-fashioned thread mittens on her wrinkled hands, Mrs Leaf bustled into the library. He asked her for the key of the schoolroom.

'The old schoolroom, Mr Dorian?' she exclaimed. 'Why, it is full of dust. I must get it arranged, and put straight before you go into it. It is not fit for you to see, sir. It is not, indeed.'

'I don't want it put straight, Leaf. I only want the key.'

'Well, sir, you'll be covered with cobwebs if you go into it. Why, it hasn't been opened for nearly five years, not since his lordship died.'

He winced at the mention of his grandfather. He had hateful memories of him. 'That does not matter,' he answered. 'I simply want to see the place – that is all. Give me the key.'

'And here is the key, sir,' said the old lady, going over the contents of her bunch with tremulously uncertain hands. 'Here is the key. I'll have it off the bunch in a moment. But you don't think of living up there, sir, and you so comfortable here?'

'No, no,' he cried, petulantly. 'Thank you, Leaf. That will do.'

She lingered for a few moments, and was garrulous over some detail of the household. He sighed, and told her to manage things as she thought best. She left the room, wreathed in smiles.

As the door closed, Dorian put the key in his

pocket, and looked round the room. His eye fell on a large, purple satin coverlet heavily embroidered with gold, a splendid piece of late seventeenth-century Venetian work that his grandfather had found in a convent near Bologna. Yes, that would serve to wrap the dreadful thing in. It had perhaps served often as a pall for the dead. Now it was to hide something that had a corruption of its own, worse than the corruption of death itself – something that would breed horrors and yet would never die. What the worm was to the corpse, his sins would be to the painted image on the canvas. They would mar its beauty, and eat away its grace. They would defile it, and make it shameful. And yet the thing would still live on. It would be always alive.

He shuddered, and for a moment he regretted that he had not told Basil the true reason why he had wished to hide the picture away. Basil would have helped him to resist Lord Henry's influence, and the still more poisonous influences that came from his own temperament. The love that he bore him – for it was really love – had nothing in it that was not noble and intellectual. It was not that mere physical admiration of beauty that is born of the senses, and that dies when the senses tire. It was such love as Michael Angelo had known, and Montaigne, and Winckelmann, and Shakespeare himself. Yes, Basil could have saved him. But it was too late now. The past could always be annihilated. Regret, denial, or forgetfulness could do that. But the future was inevitable. There were passions in him that would find their terrible outlet, dreams that would make the shadow of their evil real.

He took up from the couch the great purple-and-gold texture that covered it, and, holding it in his hands, passed behind the screen. Was the face on the canvas viler than before? It seemed to him that it was unchanged; and yet his loathing of it was intensified. Gold hair, blue eyes, and rose-red lips – they all were there. It was simply the expression that had altered. That was horrible in its cruelty. Compared to what he saw in it of censure or rebuke, how shallow Basil's reproaches about Sibyl Vane had been! – how shallow, and of what little account! His own soul was looking out at him from the canvas and calling him to judgment. A look of pain came across him, and he flung the rich pall over the picture. As he did so, a knock came to the door. He passed out as his servant entered.

'The persons are here, Monsieur.'

He felt that the man must be got rid of at once. He must not be allowed to know where the picture was being taken to. There was something sly about him, and he had thoughtful, treacherous eyes. Sitting down at the writing-table, he scribbled a note

to Lord Henry, asking him to send him round something to read, and reminding him that they were to
meet at eight-fifteen that evening.

'Wait for an answer,' he said, handing it to him,
'and show the men in here.'

In two or three minutes there was another
knock, and Mr Hubbard himself, the celebrated
frame-maker of South Audley Street, came in with
a somewhat rough-looking young assistant. Mr
Hubbard was a florid, red-whiskered little man,
whose admiration for art was considerably tem-
pered by the inveterate impecuniosity of most of
the artists who dealt with him. As a rule, he never
left his shop. He waited for people to come to him.
But he always made an exception in favour of
Dorian Gray. There was something about Dorian
that charmed everybody. It was a pleasure even to
see him.

'What can I do for you, Mr Gray?' he said, rub-
bing his fat freckled hands. 'I thought I would do
myself the honour of coming round in person. I
have just got a beauty of a frame, sir. Picked it up
at a sale. Old Florentine. Came from Fonthill, I
believe. Admirably suited for a religious subject,
Mr Gray.'

'I am so sorry you have given yourself the trouble
of coming round, Mr Hubbard. I shall certainly drop
in and look at the frame – though I don't go in much

at present for religious art – but today I only want a picture carried to the top of the house for me. It is rather heavy, so I thought I would ask you to lend me a couple of your men.'

'No trouble at all, Mr Gray. I am delighted to be of any service to you. Which is the work of art, sir?'

'This,' replied Dorian, moving the screen back. 'Can you move it, covering and all, just as it is? I don't want it to get scratched in going upstairs.'

'There will be no difficulty, sir,' said the genial frame-maker, beginning, with the aid of his assistant, to unhook the picture from the long brass chains by which it was suspended. 'And, now, where shall we carry it to, Mr Gray?'

'I will show you the way, Mr Hubbard, if you will kindly follow me. Or perhaps you had better go in front. I am afraid it is right at the top of the house. We will go up by the front staircase, as it is wider.'

He held the door open for them, and they passed out into the hall and began the ascent. The elaborate character of the frame had made the picture extremely bulky, and now and then, in spite of the obsequious protests of Mr Hubbard, who had the true trades-man's spirited dislike of seeing a gentleman doing anything useful, Dorian put his hand to it so as to help them.

'Something of a load to carry, sir,' gasped the little

man, when they reached the top landing. And he wiped his shiny forehead.

'I am afraid it is rather heavy,' murmured Dorian, as he unlocked the door that opened into the room that was to keep for him the curious secret of his life and hide his soul from the eyes of men.

He had not entered the place for more than four years – not, indeed, since he had used it first as a play-room when he was a child, and then as a study when he grew somewhat older. It was a large, well-proportioned room, which had been specially built by the last Lord Kelso for the use of the little grand-son whom, for his strange likeness to his mother, and also for other reasons, he had always hated and desired to keep at a distance. It appeared to Dorian to have but little changed. There was the huge Italian *cassone*, with its fantastically painted panels and its tarnished gilt mouldings, in which he had so often hidden himself as a boy. There the satinwood bookcase filled with his dog-eared school books. On the wall behind it was hanging the same ragged Flemish tapestry, where a faded king and queen were playing chess in a garden, while a company of hawkers rode by, carrying hooded birds on their gauntleted wrists. How well he remembered it all! Every moment of his lonely childhood came back to him as he looked round. He recalled the stainless purity of his boyish life, and it seemed horrible to him that it was here the fatal portrait was to be hidden away. How little he had thought, in those dead days, of all that was in store for him!

But there was no other place in the house so secure from prying eyes as this. He had the key, and no one else could enter it. Beneath its purple pall, the face painted on the canvas could grow bestial, sodden, and unclean. What did it matter? No one could see it. He himself would not see it. Why should he watch the hideous corruption of his soul? He kept his youth – that was enough. And, besides, might not his nature grow finer, after all? There was no reason that the future should be so full of shame. Some love might come across his life, and purify him, and shield him from those sins that seemed to be already stirring in spirit and in flesh – those curious unpictured sins whose very mystery lent them their subtlety and their charm. Perhaps, some day, the cruel look would have passed away from the scarlet sensitive mouth, and he might show to the world Basil Hallward's masterpiece.

No; that was impossible. Hour by hour, and week by week, the thing upon the canvas was growing old. It might escape the hideousness of sin, but the hideousness of age was in store for it. The cheeks would become hollow or flaccid. Yellow crow's feet would creep round the fading eyes and make them horrible. The hair would lose its brightness, the mouth would gape or droop, would be foolish or gross, as the mouths of old men are. There would be the wrinkled throat, the cold, blue-veined hands, the twisted body, that he remembered in the grandfather who had been so stern to him in his boyhood. The picture had to be concealed. There was no help for it.

'Bring it in, Mr Hubbard, please,' he said, wearily, turning round. 'I am sorry I kept you so long. I was thinking of something else.'

'Always glad to have a rest, Mr Gray,' answered the frame-maker, who was still gasping for breath. 'Where shall we put it, sir?'

'Oh, anywhere. Here: this will do. I don't want to have it hung up. Just lean it against the wall. Thanks.'

'Might one look at the work of art, sir?'

Dorian started. 'It would not interest you, Mr Hubbard,' he said, keeping his eye on the man. He felt ready to leap upon him and fling him to the ground if he dared to lift the gorgeous hanging that concealed the secret of his life. 'I shan't trouble you any more now. I am much obliged for your kindness in coming round.'

'Not at all, not at all, Mr Gray. Ever ready to do anything for you, sir.' And Mr Hubbard tramped downstairs, followed by the assistant, who glanced back at Dorian with a look of shy wonder in his rough, uncomely face. He had never seen anyone so marvellous.

When the sound of their footsteps had died away, Dorian locked the door, and put the key in his pocket. He felt safe now. No one would ever look upon the horrible thing. No eye but his would ever see his shame.

OSCAR FINGAL O'FLAHERTIE WILLS WILDE was born in Dublin in 1854. As well as several successful plays including *Lady Windermere's Fan*, *An Ideal Husband* and *The Importance of Being Earnest* he also wrote poetry, fairy stories and a novel, *The Picture of Dorian Gray*. He married Constance Lloyd in 1884 and together they had two sons, but soon after Wilde began an affair with Lord Alfred Douglas, nicknamed 'Bosie'. In a court case that attracted widespread coverage, Wilde sued Bosie's father for libel, after he accused Wilde of being homosexual. During the trial, details of Wilde's private life were exposed. He lost the case, was arrested for gross indecency and sentenced to two years' hard labour. He was released from prison in failing health and moved abroad, never to return to the UK. He died in Paris in 1900.

RECOMMENDED PLAYS BY OSCAR WILDE:

Lady Windermere's Fan
An Ideal Husband
The Importance of Being Earnest

THE IMPORTANCE OF BEING EARNEST AND OTHER PLAYS

Who would have thought a comedy of manners written more than a hundred years ago would still be so apt and so funny? Oscar Wilde was a genius of play-writing, and his deftness, wit and sharp eye for social satire keep audiences in thrall to this day. Alongside Earnest, discover a biblical tragedy retold, Lady Windermere and her infamous fan and Wilde's take on an ideal husband, in this selection of Wilde's most important plays.

'Has a strong claim to being the most perfect comedy in the English language' *Daily Telegraph*

'Remains a thing of inimitable brains and beauty; the sharpest of social satires, wrapped in the most perfect of gossamer-light romantic comedies' *Scotsman*

VINTAGE MINIS

The Vintage Minis bring you the world's greatest writers on the experiences that make us human. These stylish, entertaining little books explore the whole spectrum of life – from birth to death, and everything in between. Which means there's something here for everyone, whatever your story.

vintageminis.co.uk